M000239874

Friends Faceoff

Stephen Arnold Taylor

BookLocker
Saint Petersburg, Florida

Copyright © 2021 Stephen Arnold Taylor

Paperback ISBN: 978-1-64719-605-9
Ebook ISBN: 978-1-64719-606-6

All rights reserved. No part of this publication may be reproduced, stored in a retrieval system, or transmitted in any form or by any means, electronic, mechanical, recording or otherwise, without the prior written permission of the author.

Published by BookLocker.com, Inc., St. Petersburg, Florida.

The characters and events in this book are fictitious. Any similarity to real persons, living or dead, is coincidental and not intended by the author.

Printed on acid-free paper.

BookLocker.com, Inc.
2021

ACKNOWLEDGEMENTS

Thanks to those who contributed to improving my words in the manuscript. Tabitha Bozeman, Gail McLaughlin, Harrison Taylor for his computer expertise, and finally to Kevin Yates who saved me from drowning in computer technology.

The following contributed their expertise in helping to create the story and the plot. John Crane, former Gadsden, Alabama Chief of Police and detective, Gregory Cusimano, highly respected and reviewed attorney at law, Donald Stewart former circuit judge and practicing attorney, Sonny Taylor of Taylor Crane, Becky Noojin for her input of ideas and my daughter Stephanie Bowley for her counsel and support.

Additionally, I am grateful to all that agreed to read the manuscript and provide feedback to the author.

Stephen Arnold Taylor

4/24/2021

PROLOGUE

Phooey On Everything Tomorrow's Saturday

POETS Meeting

"Good Vibrations" rang loud and clear from the Warehouse's old rafters. Formerly a feed and seed establishment, the Warehouse had been converted to a grand restaurant and bar. It was a perfect place for the POETS Society of Riverview, Alabama, to meet.

The group was primarily comprised of long-time friends and graduates of Riverview's three original high schools: Amicalola High, Nathan Forrest High, and Riverview High. Nathan Forrest, the smallest school, was eventually closed, and students were filtered into Riverview High. Eventually, friends from the three schools noticed they all frequented the Warehouse on Fridays. Before long, running into one another had turned into regular meetings, and they began to attract members, just like social media.

The group began meeting every other Friday after work for a couple of hours to blow off steam. The friends didn't care about socioeconomic status, making for an eclectic group comprised of business professionals, food service professionals, laborers, teachers, and more. Of course, membership was invitation-only which meant you were in the social elite if you had been invited to be in the POETS group.

#

Forty minutes and several beers into the meeting, the group discussion began to get a bit off-color. Tank Wilson, the local butcher, exclaimed in response to a discussion of how size matters, "The only thing smaller than my bank account is my schlong," roaring with laughter. A couple of the women suppressed laughter, a few of the women smiled. Missy Hendricks just rolled her eyes.

JoAnn Underwood nudged Billy Mac Logan under the table. She knew that Billy Mac was the only person who could reign in Tank Wilson. Billy and Tank had played together on the undefeated championship high school team, the Amicalola Blue Devils. Tank was middle linebacker; Billy, the quarterback.

Billy Mac stood up and said, "All right everybody, it's time for our unofficial leader, JoAnn, to bring this discussion back from its present decline and present the eagerly awaited idea someone brought up at our last meeting. Silence, please! JoAnn, the floor is yours."

"What subject always comes up when we gather for our regular meetings, fellow POETS?" JoAnn began.

"Well, that subject has to be social media," said Emily Watts.

JoAnn nodded. "Bingo, Emily, social media. The greatest phenomenon of our time. All sorts of characters sounding off in different ways, from torrential political rants to slanderous remarks targeted to the fan bases of not only major league sports but also athletic programs of colleges and universities. And, what about all the pics of food, those culinary delights (or not so delightful) presented by all the chef wannabes?"

"Do I even need to mention all the personal stuff people love to share, such as grandchildren, nieces, nephews, and family gatherings?" JoAnn continued. "No longer do we need to interact with other people physically. With the internet and social media, we can now connect with hundreds of people, most of them we have never met, but we now "know" via friends of friends through our smartphones!" Age doesn't matter, young or old; social media can sure keep us occupied and addicted to our phones. However, it certainly fulfills a real need, the need to be socially accepted and liked."

She went on, "But the only thing it cannot do is to allow us to experience the intimacy that face-to-face contact with another human being brings. And that brings up the question that has spawned my idea." JoAnn paused to create anticipation.

"Damn! JoAnn! I feel like I have just heard The Gettysburg Address! What a speech," exclaimed Bobbie Jean White.

The crowd applauded, and JoAnn continued.

"Thank you, Bobbie Jean. I think I got a little carried away. The question is, how many social media friends do you personally know? How many have you never spoken to or met face to face?"

Bunches! No telling! A lot! Tons!

"How about we invite them all to a Friends Faceoff. We should have it at the Pitman Theater, which has been recently renovated by the city. It seats about 450, has plenty of parking, and still has that old theater stage where we could have a short program and dancing." JoAnn stopped and looked at the crowd.

Billy Mac rose quickly to his feet. "I move that we do it!" he said.

"I second!" said Emily.

Billy Mac called for an unofficial vote, "All in favor, say aye!"

Everyone in the POETs roared their approval.

"Listen up everybody!" JoAnn called. "We have some work ahead to make this party—which I think we should call Friends Faceoff—happen. Is it okay with everyone if I take the lead? Raise your hands if you want to have a vote."

"We wouldn't want anyone but you, JoAnn," said Billy Mac.

All hands remained down.

"It's settled then; I will take charge of organizing the event. Now we will need volunteers to plan food, decorations, and festivities. Rather than take the time now to figure it out, I'll send an email to everyone listing what's needed. If I get more than one response for each job, two can always share! Email me, no phone calls, please, with any suggestions you might have. But now, it's time to enjoy the rest of the evening and Phooey On Everything Tomorrow's Saturday!"

Everyone raised their drinks in a toast.

Chapter 1

JoAnn

It was a bright, sunny day at Berry Street Park. The sixth-grade elementary class was having a party complete with sack races, dart-throwing contests, and pole climbing. The pole had been greased heavily. The idea was anyone who could shimmy up it and touch the flag at the top would win a basket filled with Girl Scout cookies, Little Debbie snacks, jellybeans, and a five-dollar bill.

One little girl waited patiently while others tried to climb the pole.

After six people had tried and failed, the girl eyed the pole. It was time, she thought. She raised her hand, and the judge waved her on. She walked to the pole, got a firm grip, and walked her hands up the ten-foot pole with her legs providing a firm wrap-around grip. BOOM! She reached the top, touching the flag.

She won the prize. Her name was JoAnn Underwood. When asked how she was able to do that, she replied, "I waited until the six people before me got all the grease off the pole."

That was JoAnn, smart and athletic.

All of her life, JoAnn excelled in almost everything she tried. She was just one of those people with the "it" factor.

#

Years later, while attending Stanford University, JoAnn met her finance, Devon. He was a professor there but not in her department. It was love at first sight. Devon had nicknamed her "Underwood from Hollywood". He said she was as beautiful as any actress in Tinsel Town.

Two months before the wedding, Devon was tragically killed in an automobile accident; a drunk driver ran a red light. It was a very difficult time for JoAnn. She had just found out she was pregnant with Devon's child and had planned to tell him that day. Although he was gone, she was determined to raise the baby on her own.

JoAnn began to make plans accordingly when she miscarried and lost the child. JoAnn felt as if she lost Devon twice. However, she had been raised to be strong and tenacious. She continued her studies, completing a Doctorate in Behavioral Neuroscience, graduating with honors.

Right before graduation, friends invited her to a party where she met Marvin Holderfield. He was athletic, tall, dark, and handsome. He attended the University of Texas studying Criminal Justice and was visiting a mutual friend. The two hit it off, finding they had common interests, and spent the rest of the evening talking.

During the evening, Marvin told JoAnn his lifetime ambition was to become an FBI Agent and marry his high school sweetheart. She told him she intended to open a Psychology practice back home in Alabama and hoped to focus on the criminal mind.

The party ended with each swapping numbers and agreeing to stay in touch. JoAnn found herself attracted to Marvin, but she wasn't ready for a romantic relationship. Even if she was, he wasn't available. Still, a friend was always welcome in her life.

Marvin went back to Texas to finish school. He married his long time sweetheart right before he graduated and started a family not long after. JoAnn moved back home to Riverview and started her psychology practice. Her reputation grew. Not only did she attract patients from Atlanta and other parts of the Southeast, but she was also highly sought after as an expert witness in criminal cases.

# # # #

As they had promised the night they met, Marvin and JoAnn had remained friends and maintained contact for over five years. JoAnn was busy doing paperwork one evening when the phone rang.

"Hi, Marvin, it's been a bit."

"Yes, it has; time flies when you have kids!" Marvin replied. "How's your practice? Still being called as an expert witness?"

"Yes, I really love that part of my work." JoAnn nodded into the phone. "It's good to hear from you. How's the family?"

"Everyone is healthy, and so far, no one has been arrested or sent to the principal's office. You know what they say about cop's kids." Marvin chuckled. "Let me get to the reason I called besides just catching up. I could use your expertise if you are interested."

"Sounds intriguing," JoAnn replied "What do you need me for?"

"We have a serial killer in custody," Marvin continued, filling in the details for JoAnn "He refuses to speak with anyone in law enforcement. He's being held at the Federal Penitentiary in Atlanta. I was hoping you'd come and interview him, see if you can extract any information from him. I thought of you because of your interest in profiling. Normally, we don't contract out work; we use our people. But, we are way under on expenses and short on staff. I promise the pay will be worth your while with all your expenses covered. I'm figuring it'll take about three or four days, give or take."

"Email me the dates," JoAnn replied. "I'll be more than happy to rearrange my schedule. I'd never pass up an opportunity to interview a serial killer. It's right up my alley."

# # # #

JoAnn arrived in Atlanta the week following her call with Marvin. She couldn't wait to get started. She spent hours over the next few days with the suspect. He hadn't been to trial yet, but he wasn't eligible for bond thanks to the evidence against him.

JoAnn was able to strike up a rapport after reassuring him she was in no way, shape, or form in law enforcement but rather a private practice psychologist. He was thrilled to speak with her and, as if a dam had broken, began to brag about every detail of fifteen murders—not the ten the FBI was aware of. He wanted JoAnn to give everything he told her to the press. He wanted everyone to know what he'd done. He wanted fame.

Unashamedly, JoAnn led him to believe she would give the media every detail, immortalizing him along with the likes of Ted Bundy.

He was a giant of a man. And like Bundy, articulate, and well-mannered, someone you'd never suspect with one exception: he hated his mother and father. She had been a dominating woman who only paid attention to him when she was displeased. His father never stood up to her and took a lot of abuse. He blamed his son for the abusive treatment he received from his wife.

The suspect craved the attention and approval of his mother and was as abusive to his father as she was. He tortured and killed small animals and worked his way up, hoping to get her love and attention. His first human kill was his father. When that failed to impress his mother, he killed her next. He told JoAnn he loved killing; it made him feel in control and powerful. None of this surprised her; she let him believe he was in control of the interview, allowing him to brag about what he'd done. Thanks to her innate ability to connect, she was able to bring closure to fifteen families.

Thanks to JoAnn, Marvin climbed the ladder faster than many other young agents. He had been right to have her consult; the bureau even offered her a job. Although she declined the offer, his career was off and running.

#

Since Devon's accident, JoAnn hadn't dated. She poured her heart and soul into her work. Then one day, Billy Mac Logan walked into her office. He needed help coming to terms with his drinking, as well as being wrongfully fired from a job he loved.

She was very attracted to him; he was a very handsome guy, even with blonde hair. She was sure Billy Mac was attracted to her also. However, since she would never compromise her ethics or take advantage of a patient, even if he felt the same, nothing developed. JoAnn got to know Billy Mac well through therapy. He was perfect for her, the type of guy she would put aside her fear of loss to date.

Chapter 2

Billy Mac Logan: All American Boy

"Thirty-four belly right on two!" (hand clap) "Break!"

Those were the signals Billy Mac, quarterback, called. For number three, the play was for the fullback, Tank Wilson, to have the ball faked to him by Billy Mac. Then, Billy Mac could follow him through the four-hole between the guard or tackle. If there was no daylight, he would skirt around the end, but Billy Mac was confident there would be daylight. He was always confident.

Tank was a 250-pound fullback—a powerhouse of a boy. Staying low to the ground, he could easily take out two defenders and was the team's best chance of sealing another victory.

"Ready, set up, two," Billy Mac barked.

The ball was snapped. He stuck the ball in Tank's belly, pulled it out, fast, and stayed right on Tanks hips, went for two yards and a first down. Amicalola High was leading by seven with a minute left, and he could take a knee and run out the clock, but with Tank in front, he decided to take a risk. Tank knocked the middle linebacker flat on his back. Not only did Billy Mac make the first down, but he also broke free and scampered seventeen yards into the end zone.

Touchdown! That gave Amicalola their second straight State Championship.

#

The team had three outstanding offensive players. Billy Mac Logan – quarterback, Tank Wilson – linebacker and fullback, and Jeff Thomas – a big, fast, sure-handed wide receiver. They were undefeated two years in a row.

The three of them had plans after the game to celebrate. At that time, Amicalola County was dry. That didn't stop the three boys from getting beer; they brewed their own behind Tank's house. It wasn't a quick process and took about a month before it was ready to drink, but it was worth the wait. None of the boys had any idea of the alcohol content, but they knew it was much stronger than store-bought.

After the game, they headed for Tank's house and celebrated their win until the wee hours of the morning. They were the poster boys for camaraderie, were best friends, and seldom seen apart. But nothing lasts forever.

Jeff's family moved back to Cleveland, Ohio. Billy Mac went to college, hoping to leave Riverview in his rearview. Tank stayed in Riverview and worked at the butcher shop.

No one could have ever guessed what the future would hold for them.

# # # #

Billy Mac attended Auburn University on a football scholarship, but his college career was over as fast as it had started. He sustained a knee injury and never fully recovered. As a result, he decided to transfer to Jacksonville State.

The end of his athletic career weighed heavily on Billy Mac. Being an exceptional athlete fed Billy Mac's self-esteem and ego. When he lost that, he lost part of himself, and like his father, he began drinking in earnest. He was firmly on the road to becoming an alcoholic.

Life threw him some curveballs, and despite his alcohol addiction, he weathered the storm reasonably well—until his career as a cop ended, and the spiral began. That was when he met JoAnn Underwood, a woman of exceptional talents and beauty. She convinced him to attend the twelve-step program with AA, and continued seeing him until he once again had a firm footing.

Billy Mac secretly wished she was not his psychologist.

Chapter 3

The Bond of Friendship

Two days later, on Monday morning, after the POETS meeting, Billy Mac arrived at JoAnn's office. He needed to speak with her about the party and other personal matters.

"JoAnn, I really appreciate what you have done for me over the years." Billy Mac began. "The last ten years have made a new man out of me. Thanks to you and Alcoholics Anonymous, I'm proud of who I am now, and I have a successful business. So, before we get into this party planning, please let me pay you for the time you've spent with me over the years. Before you say no, this is something I've wanted to do for a long time now."

JoAnn shook her head. "Then I guess you already anticipate my answer," she replied "No. I told you then, and I'll tell you again: when I started my practice twenty years ago, I purposely budgeted time for pro-bono work, kind of a little deal I made with God. You were in need. I worked with you because I could; you were down and out and had very little money."

"Well, I wish you'd take some form of payment," Billy Mac said. "If not money, maybe a gift; it just doesn't feel right to me, not thanking you properly. I'm a successful private detective and have the means to thank you."

JoAnn gave him a look, similar to his mother when she meant no.

"Okay, okay" he laughed. "I give up." "Okay, okay," he laughed. "I give up. But, at least let me tell you how much I admire and respect you and your family without you stopping me. It must have been quite a challenge for your family to move to this little Southern City. I can't even imagine how hard it must have been to gain the white community's respect here. Although, your father being the Priest of the Episcopal Church must have helped. Of course, your mother's an amazing woman, becoming the principal of Coosa Elementary. There weren't many African American women serving as principals then. It was a time filled with prejudice and civil unrest. Still, they didn't seem to let the events of the time bother them. They persevered and earned the respect they deserved, not an easy feat in the South."

JoAnn smiled. "Thank you for your heartfelt speech. I'm blessed. Despite any obstacles that may have been present, my parents raised me to be respectful of everyone, even if they didn't reciprocate. I believe that helped many of my classmates to see the same way, at least I hope so."

"Anyway, on with the business at hand," she continued. "Thanks for volunteering to be my assistant! I have spoken with the Mayor and some council members. We can rent the Pitman for next to nothing! They just want enough to cover the utilities. They think this party will give the new venue some great exposure outside of the town's borders."

"Super!" Billy Mac said. "I think the easiest way to keep the party exclusive and manageable is for each POETS member to provide a list of people they want to invite, not to exceed 25. We'll need to ask some local dignitaries, too. Politics. I hate it, but that's how the world goes round."

"I agree." JoAnn nodded. "I think $25 per person should cover us nicely. We can provide some wine and beer, setups for BYOB, and finger food. Oh, my! Look at the time! It's time for the conference call with our volunteers."

# # # #

One Week Later

"Billy Mac, I think we're all set." JoAnn said. "Tank is providing a fantastic deal on chicken fingers and other food items, and his guy Cortez is helping him organize delivery and set-up. Missy Hendricks has volunteered to be in charge of invitations. She's going to address and mail them. I believe she's started an invitation design business and hand writes them in calligraphy. The price for the theater is $300. We'll go over all of this at the POETS Meeting Friday."

"Isn't Missy Hendricks also coordinating all invites?" Billy Mac asked.

JoAnn nodded affirmatively.

"Well," he said, "Let me know what I can do to make this party the biggest success story this town has ever seen."

####

Friday at the POETS' Meeting

Billy Mac carefully reported the progress and plans for the big event to everyone at the meeting. When he was finished, he asked if there were any questions.

Bobbie Jean spoke up, "Billy Mac, I have a question about invitations? I understand that we are each to invite up to 25 social media friends. Well, some of those will be mutual friends and overlap, is there a plan to prevent duplicate invitations? Also, the event may not sit well with some of the townsfolk because it is private; you know how people around here can be! So, I guess my question is, can we pull this off without appearing snobbish? And lastly, does the theater seat enough to accommodate our numbers?"

Billy Mac nodded thoughtfully. "Good questions, Bobbie Jean. To answer your first question, Missy has a computer program to keep the guest list straight. It detects duplicate names. How to do this without appearing snobbish? There is no way, but there is nothing wrong with a private group hosting a private party, so screw anyone that has a problem with that."

Gregory Sistern, the new President of the Bank of Riverview, raised his hand.

"Yes, Greg?"

"I would like to make an offer."

"Please do." Billy Mac nodded.

"Billy Mac, fellow POETS, I'm offering to pay all expenses for the party. Additionally, we can donate the ticket money to upgrade the town park, especially the playground. This should waylay any appearance of our group being snobbish. Although, I suspect many non-members have thought that for a long time."

There were nods of agreement and sounds of surprise as the group considered this offer from one of the town's newest residents, followed by "Wow, that's fantastic, Greg!", and "What a wonderful gesture!"

Billy Mac continued the meeting. "First, a quick vote, any problems with Greg paying expenses for the party?"

Everyone nodded with approval.

"All right, the matter's settled."

"Gregory, you are a marvel! What a wonderful offering! You should, at the very least, be recognized in some way. I propose that you and Billy Mac co-emcee," said Missy.

Greg looked at Billy Mac and shrugged his shoulders inquisitively.

"Well, as the unofficial official emcee, I think me and Greg co-host—" Billy Mac suggested. "'Course, you can emcee by yourself, Greg, if you would prefer."

"Oh, no, Billy Mac. You're the best emcee this town has!" Greg proclaimed. "I'll do it with you, though, and we'll discuss it over lunch or dinner. I would be honored to emcee with you."

Chapter 4

Planning Meeting at the Sistern's

Billy Mac placed a call to JoAnn to find out what time he was to pick her up. JoAnn answered on the second ring.

"Hello?"

"Hey, I'm calling to see what time you want me to pick you up for the volunteer meeting?" Billy Mac asked.

"Why don't you pick me up in about an hour, and we'll mosey on down there?" JoAnn answered.

"Have you ever been to the Sistern's house?" he asked her.

"Yes, several times." JoAnn replied. "I'm on the board of the little theater here, and we've met there twice this year. I've also attended a few cocktail parties there. Have you?"

"Nope. I've just seen that mansion from the road. It's got to be the biggest house in Morton Bend. Not to mention all that river frontage, it must be four or five hundred feet. It's nice of them to have an old East Riverview boy like me over to see how the other half lives, if you know what I mean." Billy Mac chuckled.

"Can you tell I'm rolling my eyes right now?" JoAnn retorted.

"Just kidding! I'm over any issues I had over being raised on the wrong side of the river!" he said.

"Very funny. Your wit is one of your strong suits." she laughed.

"Seriously, though, I'm escorting my favorite member of the POETS; see you in about 3600 seconds."

Billy Mac jumped in his car and headed over to JoAnn's to pick her up. JoAnn was ready when he arrived. As soon as she settled into the passenger seat, they took off for the Sistern's. When they arrived at the house, Billy Mac exclaimed, "Well, here we are at the mansion meeting!"

Billy Mac pulled up to massive iron gates and pushed the intercom button to announce their arrival. The enormous, iron gate opened as if by magic, revealing a majestic entrance.

They drove down the long cobblestone driveway lined with massive oak and pine trees to the circle at the end, beautifully lined with colorful flowers and flanked with carefully tended gardens.

When they got to the end of the drive, two handsome boys waved for them to stop. "Good evening, sir, we'll park your car. The golf cart is waiting to take you to the meeting room."

"Meeting room?" Billy Mac quietly said to JoAnn as they got out of the car and into the cart.

"I guess we're meeting in the large structure next to the boathouse. In all the times I've been to events here, I've never been inside the boathouse."

Waiting in the cart's driver's seat was a beautiful bubbly Asian girl who invited them to sit in the back of the cart. Once seated, she began the short one hundred thirty yards to the building.

JoAnn noticed her beautiful skin and quietly commented on it to Billy Mac. "I believe she's Vietnamese and not a day over twenty-five. She must never go out in the sun without sunscreen and a hat!"

As they got out of the cart, JoAnn and Billy Mac were each given a glittery designer bag filled with goodies. There were fine chocolates, tailgating cheeses, a jar of cookies labeled Homemade by Amanda, and a Riverview Bank tee-shirt and sweatshirt. Greg was the bank president.

"Wow, fancy for a committee meeting," said Billy Mac.

"I agree," JoAnn nodded. "But it's a nice gesture, even if it is a bit pretentious."

The couple took a quick look around before going into the building. The Sistern's had taken advantage of an old barn on the property when they bought it to build their house. The barn was close to the water and quite a spectacle. It had originally been a horse stable and had been remodeled.

Inside there were two apartments, each at either end of a cavernous common room. There were several long tables set up. Chandeliers hung from a very high ceiling, and there were two fireplaces.

It was tastefully decorated; JoAnn told Billy Mac word was that some European interior designers were involved. Billy Mac didn't answer but thought that the 5,000 square foot structure looked like a million bucks. There had to have been at least that much spent on it.

Most of the volunteers were already seated; Bobbie Jean White, a personal trainer; Hoss and Missy Hendricks, owners of Moyer Cutler Funeral Home; and Emily Watts, a former interior designer.

The last committee member was standing at the bar, doing one of his favorite things, pouring whiskey down.

Tank wheeled around and threw his hand up at his best buddy. Billy Mac waved back as he and JoAnn walked over and joined everyone at the table. About that time, Greg and his wife Amanda made their grand entrance. JoAnn quietly commented to Billy Mac that it seemed they wanted everyone to know just how wealthy were.

He nodded his agreement and noted that the boots Greg was wearing looked like expensive hand-crafted cowboy boots. Greg was tall and lanky, greying at the temples. He leaned over and said Greg was from Dallas and the son of a very wealthy Texas family, or so rumor has it. JoAnn mentioned she thought they had made their fortune in oil.

Amanda, his wife, was also from Texas. Her father had owned some kind of medical instrument manufacturing company. They bought Riverview Bank about twenty years ago.

It was hard for Billy Mac not to notice how gorgeous Amanda was and how she perfectly complemented Greg. She was tall, only a couple of inches shorter than Greg, lean, and well-proportioned. She was about eighteen or twenty years younger than her husband. They were the only members of the POETS not to have gone to high school in Riverview.

"Hey, everybody," said Greg. "Have you all got your drinks and your goody bags?"

The volunteers nodded and chanted various greetings, as well as thanks for the goody bags.

Amanda said, "Here comes something to munch on. I hope you guys are hungry!"

Once everyone had something to eat, the meeting finally got down to business. There was a discussion between the co-emcees, Greg, and Billy Mac, about their positioning on the stage. Greg said his neck turned better to the right due to arthritis, plus his right was his best side and asked if he could be positioned downstage right. He also wanted to take advantage of that position so someone could be in the wings and hold his cue cards. Greg explained how that's an actor's term that means to the performers' right as they face the audience. Billy Mac politely listened even though he knew what the term meant.

Downstage is toward the audience and where he suggested Billy Mac stand. Greg stated that although he was a bank president, he wasn't as accomplished or experienced as Billy Mac at getting up in front of others.

"I'm fairly sure whoever we get to DJ will provide mikes. Also, do you have any ideas on how the program should go?"

"First, don't worry so much, Greg, you'll do just fine. I'm thinking I'll start the ball rolling and warm up the audience for around seven or eight minutes. I'll introduce you and thank you for your generosity in supporting this event. After that, you'll speak about whatever it is you want to say, maybe even a plug for the bank. You could start by welcoming people to the party and so forth. When you're done, we'll encourage folks to mingle, eat, drink, be merry, and come up on stage to dance."

Missy asked, "What about encouraging people by having them move to different tables during the evening, kind of like Speed Dating?"

"How would we do that?" asked JoAnn.

"Well, I'm not sure." Missy hesitated before continuing. "I figured the DJ would know. I guess it might be more complicated than I thought. What do you all think?"

Amanda spoke, "Your heart is in the right place, Missy. I'm just not sure that would be manageable with a crowd that large. I believe once the program is over, the party will unfold naturally. The guests will mingle. Does anybody else have thoughts?"

"You're right, Amanda." Missy said. "I gracefully acquiesce. This party needs to, as you put it, unfold naturally."

"The alcohol will do that work for us," said Tank. Everybody laughed.

JoAnn turned to Billy Mac, "How long do you emcees see the program lasting?"

"I don't think it should be more than fifteen minutes. How about you, Greg?"

"Agreed, after all, everyone is coming to meet each other, not listen to us blab on."

Hoss spoke up, "I've hired a DJ, a fellow by the name of Jaybird—young people these days with the one name thing—anyway, he'll play some 60s, 70s, and 80s stuff. That should cover everybody there. All the folks will have easy access to the stage for dancing. When you guys are done, you can just hand your mikes back to the DJ."

"Now, how's the food, invitations, and decorations coming for the event? Tank, will you need any help with the food, and I'm sure we're all dying to know, what will you be serving?" Billy Mac asked.

"Greg told me he wants the best I've got. I've got a few guys I regularly use when I'm catering, so I don't need any help there. And, Cortez is usually available to help me with big jobs. As for food, I'm thinkin' chicken fingers; rib eyes cut small in mushroom gravy; fresh Gulf Shrimp with my special cocktail sauce; cheese and crackers, veggie trays, sour cream-based dips, and fresh hummus and guacamole to go with chips."

"Sounds like the food's under control!" said JoAnn approvingly. "Missy, what about the invitations? I would think 500 invitations, each written individually in calligraphy, is a lot for one person?

"Normally, it would be, but some of our members have graciously volunteered to help." Missy replied.

Emily Watts raised her hand.

"Yes, go ahead, Emily," said JoAnn

"I just want to report that I began planning the decorations, and they should not cost very much, and I have a couple of volunteers to help." Emily said.

"Sounds great, Emily. Greg, would it be helpful to you to have the physical receipts from everyone, or should we just shoot you an email with what we each spent?" JoAnn asked.

"Receipts would be beneficial to have for when I write the party off on my taxes!" Greg laughed. "Just kidding, an email with the amounts so I can reimburse out of pocket expenses is all I need. I'll hand out my business cards with the email address."

"I love it when a plan comes together," said JoAnn. "There is one more thing we haven't discussed, and that is the parking. Bobbie Jean, thank you for volunteering for parking duty. What kind of help will you need?

"The Evangelicals have been using the Pitman for their Sunday Worship, and a few of my young clients direct the parking for their two Sunday services. They volunteered to direct parking for us. They will also attend to any special needs of the party guests such as assisting with wheelchairs, and such." Bobby Jean answered.

"Wonderful. Well, we are about four weeks out." JoAnn continued. "I think we have a good handle on what needs to be done, and don't forget to email Greg for reimbursement."

"Greg, I'll have something for you in forty-eight hours," said Tank.

All the other volunteers promised to send receipts via email as well.

Amanda addressed everyone, "Please if any of you guys need me to do anything, let me know. Greg and I need to leave in about an hour for a previous engagement. Still, there are plenty of refreshments for everyone to enjoy. Feel free to stay as long as you wish."

"What gracious hosts we have in the Sistern's," said JoAnn. "I hitched a ride with Billy Mac, and he's given the, 'it's time to leave' signal, so thank you, guys! I know I can speak for everyone when I say how exciting this Friends Faceoff will be."

Billy Mac and JoAnn left the meeting shortly after they said their goodbyes. On the ride back to JoAnn's, they were both quiet, contemplating the recent meeting.

After they had been driving for a few minutes, Billy Mac spoke.

"Why do I feel weird?"

"That's a fastball right up there in the strike zone." JoAnn laughed. "Could it be because you are weird?"

"Ha, ha, ha, lots of laughs." Billy Mac deadpanned. "I'm sure you'll agree that we just left a party with many different personalities, but everyone was agreeable. Are we dreaming or in a movie? It's just too perfect. Seriously, do you feel that way, or is my thinking just over the top?"

"Your thinking isn't over the top at all," JoAnn assured him. "I totally get what you're saying and where you're coming from. Everyone was unusually agreeable, but then again, we are all volunteering. You know, twenty percent of people in any group do eighty percent of the work, maybe that's it, we are the twenty percent of the POETS." She paused, thoughtful, then continued. "And something else I can't figure out is Greg and Amanda's behavior; they seemed so affected."

Billy Mac nodded. "I agree. It just seems curious as to why they would come to our small town and start a bank, just out of the blue. After all, the family money on Greg's side is oil; why not go into the family business? Come to think of it, why leave Texas at all? I don't run in their social circle; normally, they are rich, but they don't act it at our bi-monthly meetings."

JoAnn laughed, "We probably are delusional. I think Greg and Amanda wanted to be successful on their own and not because they're from money, probably why they left Texas. Putting aside Greg and Amanda, we have an exciting event coming up. I'm guessing everybody senses the electricity surrounding it, and everyone volunteering is on fire. Of course, their attitude could just be for the sake of appearances."

"Could be..." Billy Mac considered it. "Back to Greg for a minute: cue cards? In the wings? For five to seven minutes? I mean, how fast is he gonna talk?"

Billy Mac walked JoAnn to the door, gave her a quick hug and peck on the cheek, and returned to his car. Time to go home and get some sleep. He was glad JoAnn had said he was ready to leave. He didn't want to be rude, after all, and it beat saying, "We're dead tired," or "I can't wait to get out of here."

Chapter 5

The Call

Billy Mac heard the song playing—it was one of his favorites, and the POETS theme song. "Good Vibrations", one of the Beach Boys most famous. They had sung it when they played a concert at Riverfest, a music festival on the river which thousands attended. For a minute, Billy Mac thought he was dreaming. He finally realized it was his phone ringing. He checked his watch; it was 6:30 a.m.

"Hello." He tried to sound awake as he answered.

"OK, QB, my hero. That left cornerback is playing me tight. A down, out and down will fake him out of his jock. What do you say, Bro? Hook me up!" said the voice at the other end of the line.

Billy Mac, a little groggy from waking up, was dumbfounded. There was a momentary silence before he said, "Jeff, is that you?"

"In the flesh Bro, your best receiver ever, at least in high school. I got your number right out of the yellow pages: Logan Investigation Services. I have been keeping up with you, Bro. Surprise! I'm coming to the party. Missy invited me. I want to see you, man, to apologize. I've found Jesus, and am a Born-Again Christian, washed in the Blood. I'm coming for forgiveness, Bro. I know I disrespected you, up and left without a goodbye, vanished. And after you tried to help me."

There was a purposeful pause before Billy Mac responded. "Jeff, you're right, you hurt me, but if you're sincere and not throwing any bull shit out there, I'd love to meet you. When are you coming?"

"Probably the Wednesday before Saturday's event; I think it's the 29th."

"When you're sure, let me know, so I clear my slate for lunch." Billy Mac paused. "I don't want to change my calendar if you're not able to make it."

"My unreliability is in the past," Jeff replied. "And, I'm looking forward to seeing you. Plus, I need to make amends to you and others. Just so you know, Missy said I could bring a guest, and I'm bringing my boyfriend, David, with me. Also, I want to hire you, but you'd need to come to Cleveland. I'll explain it all when I see you."

"I look forward to seeing you, Jeff. Bye now."

Billy Mac hung up the phone and said out loud to himself, "Shit fire and save the matches. I need to talk to JoAnn soon—yes, like today."

The text to JoAnn read: "I just got blind-sided. I'm okay emotionally, but stunned. Or, should I say downright in shock. Anyway, can we talk today?"

JoAnn replied: "Of course. Can you come by at noon? I was going to make myself a ham and Swiss cheese on rye. Can I also make one for you?"

Billy Mac sent the old thumbs-up, then put the phone aside to gather his thoughts.

# # # #

Billy Mac was sitting with JoAnn on her back porch admiring the woods and her garden. She lived in Country Club Estates, and her lot backed up to a thickly wooded area, a home to all kinds of creatures. Everything from deer to coyotes to raccoons lived in those woods. He noticed the creatures were playing havoc on JoAnn's tomato plants. When he mentioned it, she said that was the price one had to pay to grow tomatoes in your backyard.

Part of JoAnn's porch was glassed in with comfy furniture and lovely plants tastefully positioned inside, and part was screened in. They were sitting in the screened-in section. The overhead ceiling fan created a pleasant breeze. It was a sunny spring day with a beautiful blue sky, fluffy white clouds, and a comfortable 70-degrees.

"JoAnn, you've got a calming effect on me." Billy Mac said. "Between you, the breeze, and this beautiful day, I'm actually relaxing. It's helping me recover from the shock I had earlier. I almost don't want to talk about the phone call I got his morning; it might ruin this peaceful feeling."

JoAnn extended her hand toward him, encouraging him to continue.

"The call was from Jeffrey Thomas, and it threw me for a loop. I'm sure you've heard of him from the gossip mill that goes on in this small town."

JoAnn nodded. "I've heard the rumors, although I try not to take too much stock in them or gossip in general. You had touched on how Jeff hurt you during one of our sessions, but even though you never said his name, I was able to put two and two together considering the hurt he caused the town."

"I figured." Billy Mac said "I didn't use Jeff's name at the time because the hurt was still raw. One thing I'm relatively sure of is that he had an affair with my first wife. Of course, I was stepping out myself, so I didn't blame her too much. However, he was supposedly my best friend, so his betrayal hurt me worse. I don't think I deserved any sympathy, but they didn't deserve mine either. And, my wife wasn't the only woman he was seeing."

Billy Mac continued. "Then, he just up and left town with no goodbyes and after I had helped him, at least before I knew about the affair. I knew the personnel manager at the Steel Plant, I got him on there, and he thanked me by leaving, giving no notice at all. During senior year he got Missy Brown, now Hendricks, pregnant. She left town for a year or so and went to live with her aunt, which pretty much confirmed what we thought. When Missy came home, she wasn't pregnant and didn't have a baby with her. We all guessed she put the baby up for adoption. Of course, Missy never confirmed the fact."

"Now Jeff says he's a changed man, and Missy, of all people, invited him to the party." Billy Mac paused. "He says he intends to use the time before the party to beg forgiveness from everyone. He said he's a born-again Christian, supposedly gave his life to the Lord."

Billy Mac glanced at JoAnn, then back outside. "Jeff wrecked a lot of havoc in this town. Tank Wilson attacked him, and he is one powerful man. He had Jeff on the ground beating him in the face. I had to hit Tank in his Adam's apple to stop it. I didn't want to, but if I hadn't, he might have killed him."

"What set Tank off?" JoAnn asked.

"He knew Tank would be working late at the butcher shop. Jeff made sure Tank saw him buy a couple of steaks from the shop, and while Tank was working, Jeff was cooking the steaks on Tank's grill and heating things up with Genie in Tank's bed."

"Well, that would set anybody off. Do you think this guy is honestly remorseful, or is he coming to stir up trouble?" JoAnn asked.

"I don't know, the whole thing is weird." Billy Mac considered. "After all, it's been years. I didn't know he'd had any contact with Missy after high school. Maybe having had a child together bonded them. Who knows? That man can talk his way out of anything. But I'm hopeful, and I feel I should give him a chance to make amends. He was such a close friend. I'm having lunch with him before the party."

"Well, then you are doing the right thing, Billy Mac, follow your gut. I guess one thing we know for sure, Billy Mac," JoAnn paused.

"What's that?"

"All that smoothness and agreeability you were talking about earlier?" she continued.

"It's getting more complicated?" Billy Mac suggested.

"Just like social media, Billy Mac, complicated."

Chapter 6

Shaker Heights: Cleveland, Ohio

Jeffrey Thomas was making coffee. His partner, David Dingler, was still in bed. They lived in the Mother-In-Law suite behind Jeff's Aunt Sophie's home, an old antebellum home of 10,000 square feet built in the late 1860s.

Aunt Sophie was widowed. Her late husband was a General Electric Lamp Division Executive who passed away five years ago, leaving her a fifty-million-dollar estate. Four million of that was the home they renovated in 1968.

She was only eighteen then and quite a beauty. Although her husband was twelve years older, she knew what she was doing when she married him. Sophie wanted to be rich, and she had an eye for talent. She was right. Her husband, William, went right up the ladder with GE. Additionally, he made millions in real estate. Buying, selling, and developing was his hobby, and he was damn good at it.

Sophie let her deceased older sister's son Jeff, and his partner, live in the dwelling behind her home. William had built it anticipating her mother might live there one day, but she never did. The residence was 1600 square feet, with two bedrooms, two and a half baths, and a small front porch; it was perfect for the couple.

David went into the kitchen and gave Jeff a peck on the cheek. Jeff was annoyed by the kiss, but he didn't show it. He was impressed with himself for being able to fool David. Of course, maybe he was fooling himself. Anyway, he needed David to execute a plan he had in place for a while now and would only have to put up with him just a little longer.

Jeff and David could pass for brothers. Both were about 6 foot 2 inches tall, around 200 pounds, with hazel eyes and olive-toned skin.

Although Jeff was beginning to have grey streaks in his hair, their features and mannerisms were very similar, which gave away the difference. Jeff was twenty years older than David.

"Good morning, he-man, how do you like your new Keurig coffee maker I bought us?" said David.

"Out of this world. Until we get orders from the coffee club, I bought some Dunkin Donuts pods. I'll make you a cup if you do eggs benedict?" Jeff asked.

"You must have seen the Hollandaise sauce I made last night in the fridge."

"I swear I didn't, but it's music to my ears." Jeff laughed. "Hey, you know how Sophie loves your Hollandaise Sauce? Let's have her over for some Bloody Mary's and Eggs Benedict this morning."

"Sure, ring that pretty lady up!"

Twenty minutes later, Sophie was at the door and smiling. Both men gave her big hugs. They included her in their plans whenever they could. She didn't charge them rent and told them she missed her sister and just wanted to be close to whatever family she still had. And, even as a young boy, Jeff had always been able to make her smile.

Jeff mixed a tall Bloody Mary with celery and big olives, made with an overly generous amount of Tito's Vodka without asking.

"You always know how I like my drinks, Jeff. Nothing beats a good strong Bloody Mary on a Saturday morning, or make that any morning!" Sophie enthused.

"And no better company to have one with than you and David." Jeff replied.

"Well then boys, raise your glasses!"

"I'll make the toast." Jeff said. "To all of us, and the exciting adventure David and I will be pursuing, which, by the way, neither of you know about yet."

Eyebrows raised as Sophie and David exchanged inquisitive glances.

Jeff continued. "Guys, it's time I take a trip to Riverview, Alabama, my old hometown. There's going to be a big party there on May second based on social media friends. As you both know, I have unfinished business there with some folks that I've hurt. Of course, David, I'm sure it goes without saying that I want you to come with me. There are lots of things to do in Riverview to occupy your time while I'm making my rounds. Think about the fun we'll have shocking the town; I want all my old friends to know I've become who I was always meant to be, thanks to you. It would mean so much to me, what do you say?"

David got up and gave him a big hug. "I couldn't be happier! I'm especially happy for you. You're showing tremendous courage, not only making amends but taking me with you. You don't have to take me if it causes you trouble. Are you sure you want people you grew up with to know about us? I'd understand if you'd rather not come out to your old friends."

"Oh, no. It'll be fun." Jeff assured him. "I'm not sure whether to fly or drive, but driving is more romantic. In the first couple of days, I'll be making amends. But after that, I'll be all yours. We'll make everyone at the big event waggle their tongues! Food for the gossip girls. We wouldn't want to leave the people of Riverview with nothing to talk about."

"Will you be seeing anyone in particular?" said Sophie.

"No, it's an equal opportunity visit. It's time to have some conversations with my old friends."

Sophie raised her glass, "So here's to-- what's the name of the party?"

"Friends Faceoff! Cheers!"

Chapter 7

Telling Tank

Billy Mac picked up his cell phone, mashed that little bottom at the bottom, and said, "Call Tank Wilson." He heard the ring start. Tank had asked him if he minded 'Good Vibrations', too, as his ring tone. He revered Billy Mac, always had and liked to emulate him. Billy Mac told Tank that'd be great; he was honored. He knew Tank was hearing Good, good, good, good vibrations. But how good would they be once Tank heard the news?

"Hey, bud, good to hear from you. What's cooking?" Tank answered.

"Doing a little bit of this, and a little bit of that. Trying to out-hustle my competition and do a little detective work." Billy Mac replied.

"Can't nobody in my book outhustle you, noooobody!" Tank chuckled.

"Tank, I got something serious to talk to you about." Billy Mac's tone changed.

"Well, course, everything okay?"

"Yeah, nothing that can't be handled. Can I come over this afternoon?"

"Well, you know you can." Tank responded without hesitation. "How about you come to the house at about 4? I'm not working this afternoon."

"Sounds good, see you at 4 o'clock."

Tank knew something was up, and 4 o'clock couldn't come soon enough.

#

There was nobody on the face of the earth that Tank respected or loved more than Billy Mac. They met in the first grade and played marbles after school every day. The Wilson's had just moved into the neighborhood on the east side of town, and their house was right down the street from the Logan's.

Billy Mac always won no matter what they played. There was no one Tank knew who had better hand-eye coordination or athleticism. Whether it was badminton, tennis, ping pong, pool, or horseshoes, Billy Mac reigned supreme. And, when it came to any major sports such as football, basketball, or baseball, he was superior.

The only things Tank could beat him at were weightlifting and wrestling. He was State Heavyweight Wrestling champ his junior and senior years at Amicalola High. At 6 feet and close to 260 pounds, he was incredibly strong and powerful. He could bench press 500 pounds at that time without formal training.

Tank's social skills, however, were lacking, and he often struggled with interpersonal relationships. High school was the worst, but Billy Mac always protected him from ridicule, from the little giggles and gossip that flowed through the town. It was always behind his back; of course, nobody wanted to confront him face to face.

Billy Mac included him in everything he could, especially in high school. People knew not to berate or belittle him around Billy Mac. Billy Mac had a way of lifting him both socially and emotionally, and Tank had worshipped him since high school.

They were both stars on the Undefeated State Championship team. Billy Mac was the offensive player of the year in the State, and Tank was defensive player of the year; of course, Tank just needed strength and size to win that title.

They were still best buddies even though they didn't run in the same social circles now, except for POETS, and would do anything for each other.

Right at 4 p.m., Billy Mac arrived at Tank's place. He pulled to the end of the drive, where the gate to the back yard was. Tank was out by the pool and waved. He had a Budweiser in his waving hand and diet coke in the other. He was saying something, but Billy Mac hadn't heard him.

"Hey, Bud! I wasn't talking to my beer. That little ice chest over there is full of goodies for you. When you're finished here, make sure you take it with you."

"You're a big hunk of love. How many times have we been through this? You're going to go broke, giving me all that delicious food from your butcher shop for free. Let me pay you for this load."

"And just like I always say, Bud, don't steal my joy! Don't bust my bubble." Tank started chanting, "Don't give me no trouble. So what do you want to talk about?"

Billy Mac knew that the beer Tank was holding wasn't his first one.

"I don't know how to tell you this, so I'm going to give it to you straight." Billy Mac got straight to the point. "I got a phone call from Jeff Thomas, out of the blue. He said Missy invited him to the party. Insisted he's a changed man, a Born Again Christian. And he owes a lot of people apologies; says he wants to make amends! He wants to have lunch with me, even said he had some business for me in Cleveland, Ohio, where he's currently living. I told him as long as he wasn't bull shitting me, I was willing to listen."

Tank looked down and was silent. Billy Mac waited and waited and waited. Finally, after what seemed like an eternity, Billy Mac asked "Tank, what the hell are you doing? Are you okay?"

Tank looked up at him with a big grin on his face and said, "Practicing anger management." Then he burst into laughter.

Billy Mac started laughing so hard he choked on his diet coke.

After their laughter subsided, Tank said "Billy Mac, I'm alright. Don't get me wrong, I still don't like him or wanna see him, but it'll sure be interesting. You got no need to fret; there's no way Jeff Thomas is ruining this party for me."

Chapter 8

Shopping and Seeing Missy

Billy Mac had grocery shopping to do and Publix—his favorite place, especially for produce—was the place to go. They always had the freshest fruits and veggies. He was at the fruit counter looking for one of his favorites, juicy pears. He squeezed them softly to test the ripeness before buying them, just like his Mama taught him. As he was squeezing them, a female voice behind him said, "There's counseling available for your fruit fetish, you know."

He turned to see Missy Hendricks grinning ear to ear.

"Well, hello, Missy. Hey, I'm just wrestling with another one of my character flaws, I guess. You caught me red-handed. So, how's everything at the Hendricks home?"

"It's as good as it can be. Hoss spends most of his time at work, doing whatever he does down there at the Funeral Home. Then he comes home and crashes, all work and no play for that man. Of course, that means his wife gets lonely. I still like to dance, like we used to. By the way, I expect you to save a dance for me at the party."

"You know I will. I'm looking forward to it. We were quite a dance team at one time. So, speaking of the party, are all the invitations out?"

"Oh yeah, and I got a feeling everybody's coming. There's something I need to tell you, I think you should know, and I've been struggling with how. I don't want to upset you or anyone else but, since we ran into each other like this, I'll take it as a sign; I'll just spill it."

"Whatever it is, just tell me."

"Jeff Thomas is coming to the party; I invited him even though I feel guilty I did, he hurt you, not to mention the rest of the town. I was

44

going to call you, just hadn't gotten around to it yet. I need the closure we never got."

"Hey, it's okay; it's not my place to judge. I appreciate your concern, but it turns out, Jeff called me; wants to have lunch. It took me by surprise, but now I have a reason why he called seemingly out of the blue."

Missy sprang and hugged him, causing Billy Mac to blush. He would have preferred a simple bye.

"All's well in Riverview," he said. "Guess I better bag my pears and head home. See you at the final committee meeting."

Missy blew him a farewell kiss as she spun her cart around and sashayed to the checkout.

# # # #

Missy and Hoss

Missy unloaded her groceries in the gorgeous kitchen. Hoss had remodeled the kitchen for her two years ago, complete with granite countertops and brushed stainless appliances. She didn't know what that man did at the funeral home, but he sure made money. No matter, he was kind to her and generous with the money, probably to assuage his guilt.

She had everything she wanted; he bought her anything she wanted. But as the Beatles said, Money can't buy me, Love. She'd loved Billy Mac since high school. It was probably just sex to him, but then there was the affair years later. Of course, the sneaking around added excitement to the affair—what a hunk.

Hoss pulled in the driveway, entered the kitchen through the garage door, walked over, and gave Missy a peck on the cheek.

Hoss knew Missy didn't much care for him, but that was fine, as long as she didn't fuss over his vices. He was a workaholic, gambled big, hired high priced escorts, drank expensive double malt scotch, and smoked expensive Cuban cigars.

Missy always accommodated him when the mood struck him, which was infrequent, only twice a month or so. She was still one good looking woman with a beautiful mouth, expressive eyes, soft slender fingers, and an ample bosom. He liked how Missy took good care of herself. She colored her hair blond and worked out. He didn't love her, but he was fond of her.

"What's for dinner, hon?" he asked.

"One of your favorites, Missy's Chili, you hungry?"

"Yeah, but I got time for a couple of drinks and a smoke, don't I?"

"Sure, hon, go on back to your parlor, and I'll get started here."

Hoss went back and made his first drink, scotch over ice with a twist of lemon, and a little soda, emphasis on little. Hoss's drinks weren't your regular 1.5-ounce jigger; they were more like 4.5 ounces of scotch whiskey per glass.

About halfway through Hoss's second drink, he heard Missy's voice. She was loud because he usually dozed off.

"Dinner's ready!"

"Coming." He put his cigar out and left his drink. He'd come back out after dinner. He sat down at the dinner table, and she set down a huge bowl of prize-winning chili, made without beans. Hoss never did like beans.

He dug right in. He wasn't a religious man, and they never said the blessing. "Darlin' I tell you this every time. Nobody, I mean nobody, can outcook you; this is so damn good."

"Here, I buttered you some Mexican Cornbread to go with it."

The bowl she gave him was for Papa Bear. It was huge; she always served him large portions. She secretly wished he would have a heart attack. She knew it was wrong to think it; after all, he was never really abusive. He was never angry and never happy. He was a flat liner, one big lard ass bore. She frequently thought about divorcing him but liked her lifestyle way too much. She loved the pedicures, manicures, skin treatments, and had the best hairdresser and a 460 Eminent white pearl Lexus. She could support herself and probably get a sizable settlement but didn't want the hassle unless she could prove infidelity.

"Hon, I need to tell you something. Jeff is coming to the party," she began.

"I already know," he said. "We do some business at Moyer Cutler with him and have a meeting scheduled."

"Oh," she paused. "Well, did he tell you we've decided to tell our daughter who her parents are finally?"

"I want you to do what you think is best for you and your daughter."

Missy didn't respond. Hoss never seemed to care what she did. He pretty much said yes to everything.

She got up from the table, "I'm glad you enjoyed your dinner. I'm going to clean up the kitchen, take a hot shower, and go to bed. Can I get you anything else? You want some ice cream?"

"No, you go ahead. I'll get it if I feel like having any."

Missy went up to the bathroom and started the shower. She let the hot water run through her hair and down her neck, shoulders, and back. She soaped her body, feeling a tingling sensation while thinking about making love to Billy Mac; she still had the hots for him, even after all this time. She hoped Hoss wouldn't feel froggy tonight. She never knew when he would, and she wasn't in the mood to tolerate or accommodate him tonight, no matter how much money or freedom he gave her.

Missy finished toweling and blow-drying her short blond hair. She had taken her favorite comfy pajamas in with her: PJ shorts, and a long tee-shirt. As she drifted into the bedroom, she heard the good news. Hoss was snoring.

The snoring gave her an excuse to go into one of the other bedrooms. She couldn't sleep with all that noise, anyway. Their cat, Precious, followed her. Precious liked to sleep on top of her. That was fine with Missy; she'd rather have the cat on top of her than Hoss. She put the ceiling fan on low, took a sip of the Evian water by the bed, closed her eyes and drifted off to sleep thinking of Billy Mac.

Chapter 9

Contemplation

JoAnn was taking her early morning car ride. Something about being mobile always made her think better. Her friends never really understood this and even kidded her, called her gypsy woman because she liked to move around a bit.

JoAnn was one smart, confident woman, and seemingly perfect. Friends teased that she was a robot or an alien, no matter how many times she retorted she had feelings.

She was concerned about Billy Mac. The party plans were going smoothly, but now it looked like something unfavorable was being reborn with Jeff returning.

In times like this, when she needed counseling, there was always a safety net.

She turned into the driveway of her safety net, her parents. Her Dad was on his new tractor mower, trimming their two-acre tract. Mom, with scissors in one hand and a vine in the other, was trimming the tomato plants. Usually, the inside of the house belonged to Mom. It was hers to decorate as she pleased. Dad had the outside covered; the plants and trees were his domain except for the vegetable garden. She always said her Dad was rotten with tomatoes.

It was a little unusual for JoAnn to just drop in without calling. So, both her parents immediately stopped what they were doing and directed their full attention to JoAnn. John turned off the mower and dismounted as Vanessa started walking toward her daughter's car as she was parking.

"Hey, guys!" JoAnn called out. "Hugs for my crew; I need some talk therapy."

They headed inside, and JoAnn went through the whole discourse briefly. She told them how she spawned the idea for the party, and how excited everyone was about it. But, someone was about to throw a wrench into everything. This monster, this Creature from the Black Lagoon, might be a disruptive force. She had never met the creature, just had a feeling, but she was fearful, like something terrible would happen.

"So, Dad, I know the scriptures," she began. "There are so many passages telling us not to fear, but does anything come to mind for you that would be meaningful at this time? I'm feeling a bit unsettled, even fearful about this party."

"Yes, dear," he said, "but it seems to me you're more agitated than fearful, and in paraphrasing John 14:27, God tells us he gives us a peace that is not fragile like the world gives. He tells us not to worry or be troubled but to pray about everything. Tell God your needs, thank Him for His answer. Then you will receive God's peace, which is far more wonderful than the human mind can understand."

"Thank you, Dad, you always know the right passage. Here I go overthinking everything again. I guess I'm just being silly coming to talk to you guys about this."

"No," said Vanessa, "Your father and I taught you to think on your own. Of course, your Father adds the spiritual component. It's important to question things, and we're proud of the way you're concerned about others and their feelings."

"Remember, you'll always be Daddy's little girl no matter how old you get! Never stop coming to me with questions and for advice. Now come over here and get an expert Dad hug."

JoAnn stayed and talked for another thirty minutes catching up, then left for home. As she was driving, she said a little prayer thanking God for giving her the best parents in the world.

# # # #

JoAnn's phone rang. The name on her caller ID said Emily Watts, the head of the decorations committee.

"Hello, Emily," JoAnn answered.

"Hi, do you have a few minutes to talk now?" Emily asked.

"Sure do; how can I help you?"

"I wanted to report the progress on the decorations for the Friends Faceoff party," Emily began. "Everything is coming along nicely. But the real reason is to invite you to lunch. I have a friend who is enamored by you and wants to meet you. Her name is Zora Benson. She is the owner of Benson Funeral Home, the one that primarily serves the black community. Have you heard of her?"

"Well, yes," JoAnne replied. "She has a reputation of being a very sharp lady and astute businesswoman!"

"She is! I got to know her through the Businesswoman's club. I religiously attended meetings when I had my store, but now I go to meetings infrequently. By the way, why weren't you ever in that club?"

"I was never asked. I suppose psychological counseling is not viewed as a business by some." JoAnn replied wryly.

"Oh, my! A grave oversight," Emily exclaimed. "That needs to change immediately. You would add so much to that club! Would you be able to meet us Friday for lunch at the Riverview Country Club, my treat?"

"I would love to. What time?"

"Can you make it at 12:30 p.m.?"

"Sounds perfect. I'll see you there."

# # # #

As usual, JoAnn was running a wee bit late, and she was the last of her threesome to arrive for lunch. The other girls, Emily and Zora, were seated by the big picture window overlooking the golf course.

JoAnn was wearing a beautiful beige skirt that accentuated her figure with a yellow blouse flecked with orange accents. She sported a lovely pearl necklace and jade and orange earrings. Her 2-inch heels, which she usually didn't wear, made her 5 foot 9 inches tall. She was simply stunning. All eyes followed JoAnn as she advanced to meet her lunch companions. Some of the older female members of the Barracuda Bridge Club took note of her beauty and, as the name implies, sent her several jealous looks. JoAnn ignored them.

"Hi! Sorry, I'm a little late." She extended her hand toward first Emily, her hostess, then to Zora. "It's so nice to meet you."

Although Emily and Zora couldn't match JoAnn's beauty, they did look smashing. They had a radiance of class and professionalism that many can't match. They both wore elegant skirts and blouses, heels, and of course, perfectly coordinated jewelry and handbags to match. Emily wore her favorite color, a light yellow, the color of butter. Zora was more traditional with navy blue.

After some light introductory conversation, JoAnn turned to Zora, "Zora, are you familiar with Zora Hurston and her works?"

"I was named after her. My mother adored her!"

"Fabulous! So did my mother. In my early teens, she insisted I read, Their Eyes Were Watching God."

"My word, JoAnn, that's music to my ears. It's one of my favorite books. At some point, we will have to have a book club discussion."

"That's so funny. I have a good friend named Billy Mac. He and his friend Tank are huge Denzel Washington fans, and they get together and watch as many Denzel movies as they can in one night. They make such a big deal about it, like little boys who finally figured out how to skip rocks!" JoAnn laughed.

"My husband Jim, may he rest in peace, used to tell me that women don't like it when men get together and have fun."

"I remember Jim fondly. He was always an interesting conversationalist with a sharp wit and a good head for business. However, in retrospect, he was never what I'd call one who allowed himself to have fun outside the guy circle."

"He was a good salesman, though. I formulated the ideas, and Jim could always figure out how to make them work, then sell them to our customers," Zora reminisced. "We were fortunate to have done a lot of business out of that interior design shop. We made a good living, and I enjoyed that we worked together. But, like any business, it took many hours to make it successful. Probably why Jim never seemed to appreciate good clean fun."

"But hey, what about you girls?" Emily interjected. Both of you are successful businesswomen and in very different but yet fascinating fields."

Zora and JoAnn glanced at each other before Zora spoke. "Thanks for the opening Emily, I don't usually brag on myself, but this is a get to know you lunch. So, what do you girls want to know?"

"How did you get started, Zora?" asked JoAnn. "What interested you about the funeral business? And tell us a little about your journey to success. It seems fascinating."

Zora laughed. "Well, before I begin my story, I have to say that the funeral business is one with a never-ending clientele. However, as Emily said, there is a price to be paid to make a business successful, especially if you're a woman. That said, let me begin at the beginning or rather the end of high school."

"Well, it's so simple and a little weird how this all started," Zora continued. "I had an uncle who has passed now God rest his soul; he was a serial entrepreneur. He was a consummate businessman with his hand in several businesses. He did get badly burned on a real estate deal there in Dallas once, I think. But, most of what he touched turned to gold." Here, Zora paused for a sip of water.

"Well, Uncle Stoney, that was his name," she continued, "was sort of a weird guy who would occasionally throw out facts like, "Did you know that whale sperm is used to make light bulbs?" She laughed. "One day we were having a family cookout in the backyard at our house. I had just graduated from high school with honors. I was eligible for scholarships from several Texas Universities, but somehow, I wasn't interested. I did not have a clue what I wanted to do, nor a path to get there. Well, Uncle Stoney walked over to me during the cookout. He said, 'Zora, do you know how many people are in the world and how many are dead since the beginning of civilization?' 'No, Uncle Stoney,' I said. 'But I know there are several billion people in the world,' I told him."

"Yes, dear," he said. "There are about seven billion alive, and thirty-five billion that have passed on. So, Zora, what does that tell you?"

Zora laughed, remembering. "I answered that everybody is going to die. He asked, 'What else?' 'The more people are born, the more people are going to die,' I said. He said to me, 'You are on the right track, little girl, and almost all of them who die will need a decent funeral and a way to get prepared for burial or cremation.'"

"For whatever reason, that statement hit me between the eyes," Zora told them. "I knew I wanted to make money like Uncle Stoney, loved his idea, and thus found my career path. I began researching mortuary science schools and ended up going to school in Texas because it was rated number one."

"After I graduated," Zora explained, "Uncle Stoney helped me shop around for funeral homes to buy. I found that the black population was trending upward in Amicalola and surrounding counties. We heard Jessie Williams was ill and wanted to sell Williams Funeral Home. We bought it and put Benson, my and Uncle Stoney's last name on it. Gradually, we have added a white clientele, which equals about 25% of our business now. No matter their background, many people need an alternative to the higher-priced funeral homes. We found our niche and offer a lower-cost alternative to Moyer Cutler. However, we don't have a crematory; they do. So, Moyer Cutler and Benson Funeral home interchange some work. We refer cremations to them, and they send us embalming work."

Zora paused. "Okay, that's an earful about me. I'm tired of hearing myself talk. JoAnn, your turn. Tell me what Emily probably already knows about you. What's your story? How have you gained so much favor with people here?"

"You are very complimentary, Zora." JoAnn smiled. "But, to answer the second part of your question first, I assume you're saying people have said some nice things about me. Of course, one's reputation is important. I've always tried to act as my parents taught me. My father was an Episcopal Priest, and my Mom was an elementary school principal. They always told me to give people the benefit of the doubt, be respectful, but don't let anybody run over you."

"Thanks to my Dad," JoAnn continued, "my faith in Jesus as my Lord and Savior began early. Don't get me wrong; as a scientist, I've had doubts, but my faith remains strong. I want people to know that I'm open and non-judgmental, all necessary traits of a psychologist, and what I've built my business on. However, if you believe all the rumors,

I should be sainted. I do try to be honest, genuine, and forthright with people."

"Now," JoAnn laughed, "for the riveting part of my story: why I became a psychologist. At a young age, I noticed that people are different, and they've always fascinated me. My parents said that I was an extraordinarily curious child. I always enjoyed learning things. People and how they think and act interested me more than anything. There were no psychology classes at Riverview High. Still, I read everything I could get my hands on in the Public Library."

"I had a voice and academic scholarship to Birmingham Southern," she continued, "where I studied psychology. I then attended Stanford for my Master's and Doctorate, where my fascination with the criminal mind began."

Emily said to Zora, "Zora, JoAnn is immensely popular with the folks in town. In fact, she should run for mayor. I know damn well she'd win. Much like your Uncle, everything she touches turns to gold.

Emily turned to JoAnn, "I've always wondered, you being such a lady, that I've never once heard you curse. Haven't you ever thought about just letting a stream of curse words fly? It is a stress reliever for me."

JoAnn laughed, "Oh, I've done more than thought about it, even tarnished my halo at one time or another. We just don't get together enough. By the way, there are studies suggesting people who swear a lot tend to be more honest."

"Well, I must be one of the most honest people around!" Emily took a big gulp of her chardonnay that had been ordered earlier. "I guess we better order, Teresa keeps glancing over here to see if we are ready or to get us to hurry up! By the way, the sockeye salmon is divine."

"One of my favorite fish, or is it fishes?" asked JoAnn. "I feel sorry for them. You know they die after fucking?"

Emily threw her head back with laughter while Zora's mouth dropped open as she said, "Really?"

"Whoops, meant to say spawning." JoAnn made a funny face.

The girls gave their orders to Teresa. They spent the next hour eating, engaged in great conversation. As they parted ways, they vowed to get together again soon.

Chapter 10

Tank and Bobbie Jean

Bobbie Jean had spent the night at Tank's house. They had been seeing each other for over a month now. They had dated in high school; she had even worn his ring. Each had been through two marriages, but thanks to the POETS, they started seeing each other again, and she'd never been happier.

Bobby Jean had a thirty-two-year-old son who had just finished his residency at UAB in Birmingham. She was proud of Dr. Barry White; Tank didn't have any children.

"Morning, handsome."

"Morning yourself, or is it afternoon? Are you hungry? I can cook us up something delicious. I got some pork chops marinating in the fridge. I'll bring them to room temperature and fire up the grill.

"I'll make us some much-needed coffee while you are working on that," Bobbie Jean swung her long legs and put her feet on the floor. She stood up and stretched her arms and shoulders, and put on her robe.

For a fifty-four-year-old woman, she was amazing. She was willowy and slender, with a small waist and well-proportioned legs. She was in great shape.

"Baby, I've never asked, but what made you go from nursing to being a nutritionist and personal trainer?"

"Well, I decided that rather than nurse people back to health, I would rather make them healthy and not need nursing. Of course, I'd be happy to nurse you anytime!"

"Well, on that note, I'd better get a move on with breakfast, or is it lunch? One thing, I know we agreed to keep our relationship quiet until the party, but I'm just dying to tell Billy Mac. He's my best friend, and I want him to know before we show up together for the party."

"Absolutely! I believe it's time people knew I'm dating a handsome hunk. Go ahead and tell the world! But of course, tell Billy Mac first, and I'll tell my son."

# # # #

Tank Needs Advice

After Bobbie Jean left, Tank called Billy Mac, "Hey Bud, I need just a little time with you. I got something wearing me out."

"You want to come over here?"

"Yea, when?"

"Come on now. I'm free."

When Tank arrived, he sat in his favorite oversized recliner. Before Billy Mac had a chance to sit, he blurted out his news.

"Billy Mac, I think I'm in love."

"Did I hear you, right?"

"Don't make me say it again. I'm as happy as I have been in a long time, but I'm scared shitless."

Billy Mac responded with his Richard Nixon impression. "Well, as you know, Tank is it? I am an expert on relationships." He slipped into Donald Trump, "As far as relationships go, I know all about 'em. It's incredible what I know. Dr. Phil and Oprah can't hold a candle to me. I am simply amazing."

"Come on, Billy Mac!" There was real concern in his voice.

"Oh, I'm sorry, Bud, didn't mean to make light. Who is it that has you in a tangle?"

"It's Bobbie Jean. We started hanging out after the POETS meetings, and just like in high school, flames started flying. I'd do just about anything for her, anything! That's love, isn't it?"

"I was kind of making fun of myself a while ago. Remember what I've told you about my previous relationships? Or I should say, a lack of relationships; sex is not a relationship. I was like a milk carton, thinking I was well past expiration. I thought it was time to give up on having a meaningful relationship."

"Well, she's put a spell on me. She says I make her laugh, go figure."

"I'm happy for you, bud. Course, I know one thing."

"Okay, I'm biting. What?"

"You're never gonna understand her! In general, understanding women is an art form that I believe men are never going to perfect.

So, stop selling yourself short. You're a great guy! If she loved you in high school, why not now? Maybe you didn't go to college, but she wouldn't be dating you if that was important to her. You make me laugh too!"

"I knew you'd put everything in perspective. I'm still scared shitless, though; it all seems too good to be true. I'm afraid I'm gonna wake up and find out this is all just one beautiful dream."

"Hey, being scared is part of the deal; we can't predict the future. Just enjoy what you have now, and as I've heard JoAnn say many times, just go with the flow."

Tank left to go back to butchering at his shop, leaving Billy Mac to his thoughts.

# # # #

Call from Missy

Suddenly the Beach Boys were playing, pulling Billy Mac out of his thoughts. He picked up his phone and saw Missy's name on the caller ID. "Damn." He let it ring three times before deciding to pick it up. "Hello, Missy."

"Do you have time now to talk a minute? I need your help."

"I'm working on a couple of cases keeping me real busy, but sure, I got a few minutes. How can I help?"

"Logan Investigative Services are needed by me. I want to tell you up-front, I don't want any special pricing. I have plenty of money and want to hire you. I'm pretty sure, almost positive, Hoss is cheating on me, often. I just need proof, in case I decide to take him to court."

"What makes you think he's cheating?"

"All sorts of suspicious things. For instance, he recently lost his phone. There were a bunch of numbers I didn't recognize. I figure they must be women after my friend, who works at the dry cleaner's, told me he's been sending shirts there with lipstick marks. There's other stuff, but I'd rather talk to you in person, and I need you to start as soon as possible. I'll give you a stash upfront."

"Where do you want to meet?"

"It's a way off, but let's meet at Mt. Cheaha. That way, Hoss or his cronies won't see us. You know where the overlook is by the hotel? There is a big parking area there."

"I know where that is, what time."

"Can you meet in the morning, around 10 o'clock? I'll be in the white Lexus."

"Yes, I'll pull up beside you. I have a black Tahoe."

"See you tomorrow Billy Mac."

"See you."

Son of a biscuit eater! Billy Mac thought.

# # # #

Call from JoAnn

There go the Beach Boys again. Maybe this time, it really would be good vibrations. He looked at the caller ID; JoAnn, thank you, Jesus! "What's going on in the underworld of Underwood?"

Her voice sounded concerned, "I feel like I'm upside down."

"Well, you know what Confucius says about that?"

"What?"

"Never mind, what's wrong, Joann?"

"Role reversal, my friend. This time I need a counselor bad. I'm on a rocky cliff and feel like I have no rope. Can you come over, or do you want me to come over there? On second thought, Billy Mac, please come over here. I need to pour myself a large glass of chardonnay, and I know you don't keep libations in your house."

"I can come right now."

"Great, I'll be on the screen porch."

Billy Mac wasted no time. When he arrived at JoAnn's, he pulled to the end of the driveway and quickly headed for the screened-in porch. He hadn't even taken time to change and was wearing what he had on that morning, cowboy boots, jeans, and a long-sleeve denim shirt with his white polo tee-shirt showing underneath. He was an extraordinarily good-looking man at 6 feet 3 inches tall and 210 with boots on. He had light blues like Paul Newman and thick wavy locks of blond hair, and no grey.

JoAnn waved him in. She was wearing a Stanford sweatshirt with red lettering and dark red Bermuda shorts. Her sandals, earrings, and bracelet matched the shorts perfectly. Even upset, she was put together. Beside her on an end table was a glass with a little ice and a lot of caramel-colored liquid.

"Is that a new chardonnay?"

"No," she said as she raised her eyebrow, "but it starts with a C, Chivas Regal."

"I thought I recognized it. Now you know my counseling sessions don't come cheap. My price is steep, a diet coke."

JoAnn snapped her fingers, reached down on the floor beside her, and voila, rescued from its hiding place a tall glass of diet coke and ice, poured from a bottle, and handed it to him.

"Thank you, my dear. I see you were ready for me."

JoAnn had been sipping on her scotch. She now took a big gulp, then another big gulp, and burped accidentally. She smacked herself in the chest, "My word! Excuse me."

"You're excused, but the price for being excused is you must now dance on the table."

JoAnn jutted her chin out like royalty. Holding up her hand, palm toward her, bellowed, "War Eagle, five times as powerful as the bird," as she said the bird, she folded down her thumb and other three fingers so that the middle finger became prominently displayed.

"That Chivas is good medicine, now what is this all about?"

"I'm usually brave, don't you think? But in the last few days, I've been feeling a bit scared."

"You're as courageous as they come. We all get scared. You wouldn't want Stephen King to be out of a job, would you? He scares me."

"Me too! But seriously, I've been receiving anonymous emails saying the POETS are gonna be sorry for being such snobs, and we all need to watch our step. The most recent was downright hateful, threatening me specifically. I know lots of people think we're snobs, but I had no idea our invitation-only party would draw this kind of ire from the townspeople."

"How long has this been going on?"

"Oh, not long, less than a couple of weeks. I wasn't worried, but recently the emails have a definite threatening tone."

"I'm going to find every son of a bitch doing this."

"Let's wait and see. I suspect it's more than one person, but I don't think anything will come of it. Normally I wouldn't let it bother me; after all, there's always going to be haters. But I have a serious health concern that's throwing my hormones out of kilter. I've been depressed and extremely emotional. I have not told anyone about this, including my parents."

"Okay, go on."

"There's a knot under my breast and something in the lymph nodes. It's been biopsied, and I'm awaiting results. They think it could be cancer."

JoAnn started tearing up, and Billy Mac felt a lump in his throat. He sprang to his feet, sat by JoAnn on the sofa, wrapping his arms around her as he cradled her head on his shoulder. She began to sob silently. He stroked her hair and put his face up against her forehead, feeling the wetness of her tears, her body gently trembling against his. He hated seeing her like this.

Billy Mac silently held JoAnn for about ten minutes but would have held on for eternity. Finally, JoAnn slowly regained her composure. She placed her hands on each side of his cheeks and pulled him toward her as she kissed him on the lips with subdued passion.

"I'll be right back. Give me your glass, and I'll bring you some more diet coke."

Billy Mac said nothing as she walked to the bathroom. He heard the water running and the toilet flush. In a minute, JoAnn reappeared with more diet coke and ice. She sat down beside him, but they were no longer touching, though there was an electric tension in the air. They talked for about an hour.

Finally, Billy Mac asked, "Do you want me to stay here with you tonight?" He knew he was taking a leap of faith. After all, the kiss may just have been because he was in the right place at the right time, and she was upset.

"No, I'm all right. You've been a huge help. I couldn't ask for a better friend. Oh, before I forget, we've been invited to the Sisterns' house, just the two of us, Friday night for dinner. I believe they think we're a couple. Anyway, Greg wants to talk to you about his inaugural debut as Master of Ceremonies. I think he's pretty nervous. Plus, it'll give me a chance to get to know Amanda beyond our bi-monthly meetings."

"Sounds like fun. Better be on my way. It's getting late. Keep me posted on those emails. I'll do whatever it takes to protect you from threats and get you well."

"I know."

She reached up and kissed him again firmly on the lips.

"I'll call you if I need you. Thank you!"

As Billy Mac walked out, she said to herself, you liar, you did want him to stay.

Billy Mac got in his Tahoe, shut the door, and said out loud, "Son of a Bitch." A range of emotions swept over him, fear, hope, anger, happiness, pure joy, and love. It seemed as if a dream was coming true.

Their relationship had evolved to a different level. He didn't know what level, but he did know one thing for sure, he was in love with JoAnn.

Chapter 11

What happens in Vegas stays in Vegas

Hoss and Greg had met at a National Funeral Directors Association Convention in Las Vegas. Greg was a financier, an extraordinarily rich one, and wanted to invest in the lucrative funeral business. Texas Oil had made his family rich; his inheritance had made him rich. He was there at the convention looking for investments and gambling.

Hoss had hatched quite a scheme to enhance the already profitable side of the funeral business, and Greg eagerly invested. And now, eighteen years later, they were getting ready once again to embark on a trip to Las Vegas. They were set to leave in a few days for the annual National Funeral Directors Association Convention.

Making money was a game for Hoss. Greg was an artist at heart. The only thing they had in common was their business holdings. They spoke in code when they discussed business affairs as if what they were saying was being overheard. They derived extreme pleasure from this conversing method, believing it created deception for the covert activity they engaged in. This was important to Hoss, and easy-going Greg went along.

Hoss had called Greg, "Well, I understand the bear trap has been set for the Grizzly with Mama's cub as bait."

"The plan is in place."

"What about our tickets to Vegas, that all set?"

"Yea, my secretary Dot bought us three seats in first class. That will give us plenty of room with that middle seat open, not to mention the two extra free drinks per seat for you."

"Great. I've got some new people for us to meet. People that deal with financing matters much akin to us."

"Always interested in meeting new ones, keeping our way of operating fresh. As we fly out of Birmingham, do you want to drive down there Sunday or get our wives to take us? Amanda said she'd like to see us off."

"Let me think on that. But I reckon it would be fine if Missy and Amanda took us."

"I'll call you Saturday."

# # # #

Meeting Missy at Cheaha

While Hoss and Greg met to discuss the convention, Billy Mac was on the way to meet Missy at Cheaha.

Billy Mac enjoyed the scenery as he traveled up the wooded mountainous road. Cheaha was the highest point in Alabama, and he was meeting Missy at the overlook. It was such a beautiful drive.

Missy was early. She pulled into the parking lot and parked at the end of the paved area with the glorious view below. In ten minutes, she saw the black Tahoe pull into the lot and park next to her.

Billy Mac parked next to her passenger side. He opened his door and slid in beside her. "Greetings!"

"Thanks for coming. As I said over the phone, I need proof that Hoss is cheating. Hoss has always cheated on me. I think I've been a convenience to him for a long time, keeping him respectable. He's a strange man who doesn't seem to have feelings for anyone but himself and money. He just uses and manipulates people. Don't get me wrong, he's not abusive to me, but we have no intimacy; that's one of the reasons I suspect he's cheating. Plus, he goes out at all hours of the night after receiving phone calls.

I've started my own business designing and customizing invitations. That's why I volunteered to do the invitations for the party. The business gives me a purpose and an income. I have plenty of money put aside to support myself and how I can pay you without Hoss finding out.

I've also received a few threatening emails saying the POETS are gonna be sorry, and I'll be sorry if my past comes out. I need you to look into them. It's making me worry something terrible is going to happen that night.

There's something I want you to know, in case something does happen to me. I'm sure you and the whole town knows that Jeff got me pregnant. My parents sent me to an Aunt in Texas, where I had the baby and gave her up for adoption. That baby married Greg. What are the odds that my daughter would end up right back in the town she was conceived, right? Well, I know she's been researching who her biological parents are. She told me she wants to meet them, to know where she came from. I've wanted to tell her for years, but the bastard refused; he didn't want to meet her. For whatever reason, only God knows, he's finally agreed to telling her. That's why I invited him to the Friend's Faceoff Party, and that's why I'm nervous about the emails."

"Whoa, that's an earful. Greg and Amanda have invited JoAnn and me over tomorrow night for dinner."

"I know. Amanda and I are good friends, weird, right? At least I've had a relationship with her, though I'm afraid of losing it once we tell her the truth. Anyway, she told me about dinner and that Hoss and Greg are off to Vegas for the Funeral Directors Convention this Sunday."

She reached into her purse and handed Billy Mac an envelope full of Benjamin's.

"I'm positive there will be women involved in this trip, so you should get the proof I need fairly easily. I've bought a pre-paid cell. I don't want to take any chances of Hoss finding out. The number's inside the envelope. That's it, in a nutshell."

"I'm happy to take your case. You deserve better than a cheating husband."

"I don't know, and really, I don't think so, but those emails are creeping me out. What if Hoss is sending them to threaten me? He might suspect I know about his infidelity. But Hoss is a spooky man. Sometimes he can be downright creepy with his going out at all hours, not telling me about any of it when I ask. I just got a feeling."

"I'll get to work. Just one more thing, we need to find a more convenient place to meet, it's a scenic drive but way too far for a short meeting! I'll be in touch as soon as I know anything. In the meantime, be careful."

As Billy Mac began the thirty-five-minute drive back to town, his thoughts turned to JoAnn. The Big "C" scared everybody. It may be nothing, and he prayed that be the case, but he was worried. Their relationship began when she was his counselor, and somewhere along the way, they became good friends. They were just beginning something special. He just couldn't bear to lose her.

His thoughts wandered back to Missy. He pondered his assignment and didn't want to keep the fact that Missy hired him from her. After all, he does have a past with her. He was trying to think of how JoAnn could be in the know and not compromise his integrity or client confidentiality. He knew one thing for sure; he was looking forward to their "date" tomorrow night at the Sistern's.

Chapter 12

Friday, 2 pm: Love in the Making

Billy Mac put in a call to JoAnn. She answered on the first ring.

"Hey, what time should I arrive?"

"Why don't I pick you up?"

"Why? Men don't ride in Volvos, do they?"

"Oh, it's exciting when your fangs sharpen. I know I'm in for a wonderful evening of biting humor."

"I'll try to have them sharpened and cleaned. I just bought a new electric toothbrush, with a sharpener today to do just that. You know, it sounds like fun to be picked up by a beautiful girl."

"Okay, it's settled then. We need to leave your house at 6 o'clock, so I'll see you a little before then. What are you wearing?"

"You tell me, after all, you're the fashionista and expert on dinner invitations. Should I wear a sport coat?"

"Yes, I believe so. I'm sort of seeing this as a dress rehearsal for the main event. But not too formal, something sporty."

"Gotcha! I was thinking the same thing. See you in a few."

I wonder why she wants to pick me up, thought Billy Mac. Maybe I'm old fashioned, but in my experience, the guy always picks up the girl. Well, no mind, I better get moving so I'll be ready.

#

JoAnn arrived at 5:45, wearing an exquisite summery maxi dress. The sleeveless top was white with a deep V, allowing a tasteful but sexy peak of her breasts. The skirt was black with a pink and white floral pattern and a slit that revealed a tantalizing view of her long, gorgeous legs. She was absolutely stunning. It was quite a departure from the professional suits she wore in the office.

Billy Mac was blown away. He simply could not hide the emotion on his face.

"I have never seen anything more beautiful. I think I need a respirator."

JoAnn kissed him on the cheek, then she threw her arms around him and gave him a big hug. She had her little cocktail suitcase, virtually a traveling bar. Billy Mac invited her in.

"I'm making myself a stiff drink before we go."

She set the case and her purse down on the table and reached in for her keys to hand them to Billy Mac.

"Will you be my Uber?"

"Sure, Madame. Of course, I'm a Lyft man myself. You know, like Denzel was in Equalizer II."

They both had a good laugh over that one.

"Billy, you look pretty smashing yourself. You are one handsome man. I love that coat and shirt on you."

Billy Mac liked it when she dropped the Mac. She was the only one that did that, and only occasionally. Somehow it made him feel more special.

Billy Mac's coat was a checkered pattern of pinks and blues. He was wearing a white silk shirt open at the top with no tee-shirt and light cream pleated pants. He had on slip-on Mephisto Loafers, brown, with thin cream socks.

It would be hard to find a better-looking couple, even in Hollywood.

JoAnn mixed a gin martini, straight up, with a whisper of Vermouth and two big fat olives.

"We've got a spell. We really don't have to leave at 6. Greg and Amanda said to come at 7. You sure you're okay if I have a drink?"

"I'm sure. In fact, I would've fixed it for you. I literally have no cravings for it, as long as I don't take a taste. I'm glad you came early, and we got some time. More importantly, I'm glad you're feeling better and in seemingly good spirits. Not to poke the bear in the room but have you gotten any more of those emails?"

"Not at this point. As for my health, things are in God's hands. I truly believe that as long as I trust in Him, I'll be all right. I feel great. I went for a run this morning, plus I got one hell of a good man watching my back. That would be you, in case you weren't aware."

"You're an extraordinary woman, JoAnn."

JoAnn set her drink down. Billy Mac was sitting on the sofa, and she moved to sit next to him, turned, and put her legs up with her back to him. She leaned back and put her arms around him and planted her lips upon his. This was the first real, meaningful kiss they had ever had. It had been building for years. No more platonic relationship; they had officially moved on. This romance was real, and the kiss was passion unleashed, like a bucking bronco coming out of the gate at the rodeo.

After several breathless minutes, Billy Mac picked JoAnn up and carried her to the bedroom. They made mad, passionate love for forty-five minutes. Billy Mac and JoAnn were experiencing the most memorable evening either of them has had in years. They reluctantly got up to shower, redress, and managed to arrive on time at 7:30.

The 15-minute ride to the Sisterns' was very romantic. JoAnn wanted the sunroof back and sat as close to him as the bucket seats would allow. A gentle breeze caressed them as they drove.

It was apparent that they were two people in love, probably had been for a long time.

JoAnn was thinking about how she had not made love or allow herself to fall in love for years. She had been cautious after Devon was killed years go in the car accident. She was afraid she would be unable to handle something like that again and didn't want to be hurt.

She had loved him deeply, but she was ready for love. And, now she loved Billy Mac as much and probably more. It was time to release the song "Music of the Night" from Phantom, "Silently the senses abandon their defenses." She had abandoned her defenses and opened herself back up.

They drove down the long tree-lined drive and pulled around the big Colonial mansion's circular drive in front.

The door opened, "Welcome, Oh! What a smashing couple! Hey Greg, we have people from Hollywood here." She called over her shoulder.

"You're too kind. Of course, this is like a Hollywood set; you have such a majestic home. You look great, Amanda. I see you maxi dresses are in for the evening."

"Got it at Kohl's. Course it was a bargain, on sale, always a good reason to buy, don't you agree, Billy Mac?"

"Absolutely, Amanda! Why would you let those "on-sale" dresses hang around the store when they could be hanging in a better place, your house, or even better, on you."

JoAnn pinched his cheek.

"Now you're catching on, Billy Mac. Why you men actually might start shopping sales like us girls, do!" She winked at Amanda, who chuckled.

"Come on, let's go to the den."

Greg had a lanky stride, which was even more pronounced by the white pants he wore. Over his sloping shoulders, he had on a beige cashmere sport coat. Greg walked out of the den and motioned them in. He had an emerald ring around his little finger and a gold chain around his neck. He was at least twenty years older than Amanda, flashier, and really, blue suede shoes? Billy Mac kept his thoughts to himself.

Greg shook hands with Billy Mac and JoAnn.

"Sit wherever you're comfortable. I'm taking drink orders."

JoAnn had sat down beside Billy Mac on the big leather sofa. She nudged him with her leg and replied, "Well, I started earlier with a Martini I didn't get to drink as we were running a little late, so why don't I just try again. Straight up with olives."

"Billy Mac?"

"Got any ginger ale?"

"I most certainly do, over ice?"

"Over ice is perfect."

The evening went smoothly. The Sistern's were easy to talk to. There was no pretense about them tonight. He and JoAnn had observed a different side of them at the committee meeting. Billy Mac found that he liked Greg, though he didn't think he would. He seemed like an okay guy.

Probably because he ordered a soda, the conversation turned to sobriety and the twelve-step program. He told Billy Mac that he had done the twelve-step program with Gamblers Anonymous.

"I guess that is not the best character flaw for a banker to have. I'm supposed to be protecting people's money, but I swear I never used client money. I still do some gambling, but nowhere near what I did in the past. In fact, Hoss and I are leaving for Vegas Sunday. There's a Funeral Director's Convention."

"It's admirable you don't fall back into your old habits if you still gamble. I know if I have just one drink, I would slip and fall faster than a penguin on ice."

Of course, Billy Mac knew about the trip, Missy had informed him. He would be working that trip in some form or fashion, not that Greg or Hoss would know.

Billy Mac viewed Amanda in a new light. Although she had terrific adoptive parents and rich ones at that, he felt sorry for her. He hoped that Jeff could enhance her life when they broke the news to her along with Missy. She looked more like her father than Missy, but she seemed to have Missy's mannerisms and personality. Billy Mac noticed that Amanda and JoAnn seemed to be hitting it off. Who wouldn't like JoAnn?

Before dinner, Amanda invited JoAnn on a short tour of the house and suggested Greg do the same with Billy Mac. They set off in separate directions.

As Amanda led JoAnn, they entered a large study/office with a giant aquarium filled with beautiful tropical fish varieties. On the shelves of a grand mahogany desk were two books and a screenplay. Ayn Rand authored the screenplay and book. They were the classic novel Atlas Shrugged and The Night of January 16th. The other book on the desk, prominently displayed, was The Joy of Sex.

Amanda noticed JoAnn looking at the books, not in the least embarrassed by anything in view.

"As you can see, I am a fan of Ayn Rand. Have you read her?"

"I have read Atlas Shrugged and seen the play The Night of January 16th. I've also seen an extended interview with her on the old Phil Donahue Show."

"Oh, I guess I just assumed you being the daughter of an Episcopalian Rector, you wouldn't be a fan."

"I'm a fan of capitalism, which she touts in Atlas Shrugged; but, I am not a fan of objectivism. I don't believe that the moral purpose of life is the pursuit of one's happiness. I believe in showing and practicing compassion for others. From what I have garnered, she does not and is an atheist, believing faith to be a natural detriment to reasoning. I believe in God, Jesus, and having faith."

Amanda smiled and quickly changed the subject. They continued their brief tour. Meanwhile, Greg and Billy Mac were viewing some of Greg's paintings.

"If it were up to me, Billy Mac, I would do nothing but paint. Ever since childhood, that has been my true passion."

"Well, you should do more of it. From what I see, you're very talented."

Amanda's voice echoed through the house.

"Come on, guys, dinner time!"

The dinner was fantastic; Greg and Amanda had gone all out. The first course was a seafood gumbo. Billy Mac could swear it was fresh from New Orleans. The second course consisted of Fresh Red Snapper, and Pork Tenderloin sliced very thin, rice, green beans, and delicious flaky rolls. For dessert, a caramel-covered upside-down pineapple cake was served with coffee.

After dinner, Greg mentioned he was nervous about standing up and speaking in front of a large group but thought he would do okay as long as he had his cue cards. Billy Mac expected more discussion than that about their gig at the party, but there was none. Up to that point, the conversation hadn't touched on the party.

A few minutes after coffee and dessert, Billy Mac and JoAnn said their goodbyes

"That was lovely, much better than I expected; they seemed different than they had at the committee meeting, or even at the POETS meetings. Although I did expect more talk about the party."

"So, did I? I guess he's not as nervous anymore. Earlier in the evening wasn't bad either."

"Well, you know what I've got to say about that."

"No, but I bet you're going to tell me."

"Shit, fire and save the matches!"

Billy Mac laughed deep from his belly, "Hey, that's my line."

JoAnn reached down and placed her hand on his legs and leaned in.

"Well, since our relationship is at a new level, I can use some of your material."

"Ummmm, yes, makes sense, okay, I give."

"Billy?"

"Yes?"

"I would like if you would stay at my house tonight. I can take you home in the morning."

# # # #

Their lovemaking lasted until the wee hours. Exhausted and fulfilled, they slept soundly until 8:30 the next morning.

When JoAnn awakened, she heard the toilet flushing and water running in the master bath. She got up and pulled on a pair of gym shorts and a Fleet Feet tee-shirt.

When Billy Mac came out, he was in his underwear. He smiled. "Good Morning. I used one of your new toothbrushes."

"Good! I was going to tell you there was one in there; I always keep extras."

Billy Mac walked over to the chair and slipped on his pants and shirt.

"You up for a big breakfast, or do you want something light? I'm heading to the kitchen. I make a mean omelet, and I got some of Tank's home-grown sausage."

"Okay, big breakfast, it is. What about coffee? Did you set the timer last night?"

"Yes, it should be ready. Go on and pour yourself a cup while I take a shower and get ready."

Thirty minutes later, they were eating on the back-porch Billy Mac enjoyed so much.

"Your appointment with the oncologist at UAB is this coming week, right?"

"Yes, Wednesday at 10 in the morning. Can you take me?"

"Of course, I was hoping you would ask."

The rest of the meal conversation centered around their evening at the Sistern's. Billy Mac's thoughts wandered to how he could tell JoAnn Missy had hired him.

JoAnn took Billy Mac home at 11 a.m. Before getting out of the Volvo, he leaned over and gave her a light peck on the lips.

"JoAnn, did I tell you that I was madly in love? I don't think it would be healthy to keep anything from my counselor."

"Thanks for sharing, Billy Boy. I'm in love too, with a member of the POETS society, a big hunk of love named Billy Mac Logan. Have you heard of him? I'm head over heels in love and happier than all get out."

He stared at her a minute as tears of joy welled in his eyes; this was the first time they had acknowledged being in love. He squeezed JoAnn's hand.

"I gotta go, got some work to do. I'll call you later today."

JoAnn nodded while smiling. She threw him another kiss and drove off.

Chapter 13

Billy Mac Calls Missy

Billy Mac had put Missy's new cell number in a safe place, his head. He was very good at remembering phone numbers. The area code and exchange were two numbers to him because they were familiar. So, the last four numbers were all he needed to remember.

"Hello, Billy Mac. How did the evening go?"

"The evening was nice. I must confess I looked at Amanda in a different light. Missy, she has many of your mannerisms and your style. There is just something charismatic about her, do you know what I mean?"

"Oh, yes! Can you imagine how hard it's been being her friend and her mother without her knowing I'm her mother?"

"I can only imagine Missy. But that has everything to do with why I called."

"Amanda and JoAnn seemed to really connect, and I thought you might want to consult with her before you and Jeff drop the bomb to Amanda. She's a great counselor, and she may have advice on how to handle delivering the news. Apart from that, I'd like permission to let her know you've hired me to look into the emails you've received and, of course, tailing Hoss. I've consulted with her in previous cases, and her expertise helped close those cases pretty quickly. I'm not asking for additional money. I'll take care of any additional fee consulting her incurs. What do you say?"

Missy was silent for a few seconds. "I must admit, Billy Mac, I was not expecting this. This information is very personal. I've given you information I don't want to be leaked to the gossip girls. I trust her professionalism, but I'm just trying to prove my bastard husband's cheating. Do you honestly think we need to consult her?"

This time Billy Mac was silent for a few seconds.

"Missy, I guess I should've told you about JoAnn when you hired me. She's a silent partner and partly the reason for my success. I should've been upfront and let you know that I discuss all my cases with her, even simple ones with bastard husbands. Another thing, I'm not feeling comfortable surveilling Greg while surveilling Hoss. We've got a tentative friendship due to being co-emcees and all, plus I like him. It's a strange set of circumstances. I'd like to keep working for you, especially regarding the threatening emails, but you can always hire someone else. I've no problem returning your money."

Missy sighed, "I appreciate you're telling me this. Of course, I don't have a problem with JoAnn knowing. I trust both of you to be professional, and Hoss, he's a strange one. JoAnn's insight may just further my cause if I do divorce him."

"You're probably right about that! I'll be back in touch soon."

Chapter 14

Cortez Cortez

Cortez emigrated from Cuba when he was a child. His family name is Ramos, but since he's not a citizen, he never uses his legal surname, harder for Immigration to catch up with him. Even though he never obtained citizenship, he's worked since he was a teenager. He's been with Moyer Cutler Funeral Home for years and works part-time for Tank at the butcher shop. Tank's often asked him what he does at the funeral home and repeatedly told him he could run circles around him with a knife.

Tank and Bobby Jean were enjoying a beer on his deck when the Beach Boys rang out. A glance down showed Cortez was calling.

"Hey, Buenos Diaz." Tank put him on speakerphone.

Cortez's English was still broken and heavily accented even after years in the States. "Tank, you and I talk, okay?"

"Okay, Cortez, on the phone or in-person?"

"No, you see me."

"Sure, alright. Where should I meet you?"

"Back of the store? Okay?"

"When?"

"Now, por favor, I see you now."

The phone was on speaker, and Bobbie Jean nodded approvingly to Tank.

"Okay, twenty minutes?"

"Si, goodbye."

Tank looked at Bobbie Jean. "For fifteen years, that boy has worked for me, and he's never called before. It sounds urgent, and he seems almost scared, doesn't he?"

"Sure does; go see what he wants. I'll wait here for you."

# # # #

Twenty minutes later, Cortez was standing at the back door of the store when Tank arrived. They exchanged greetings and went into Tank's office to sit down.

"I want work here, for you." Cortex began.

"Well," Tank replied, "I have some work coming up for you soon, the big party is in two weeks, and I can give you several hours."

"I work with you all the time, all the time, every day."

"You mean you'd leave the funeral home? That's good pay, Cortez."

"Demasiades gente muerta!"

Tank thought he knew what Cortez said, but he repeated it to be sure, "Demasiades gente muerta?!"

"Si, dead people, lots of dead people."

Tank Googled it to make sure he understood him, "too many dead people."

"I need to think on this. I don't see how I could give you a decent wage; you know, mas dinero."

They talked for another twenty minutes. Cortez was insistent and said over and over he would take less money than he was making now. They shook hands, and Tank said he would call him soon. He let Cortez out, locked up, and went back home to be with Bobbie Jean.

Chapter 15

Phoning Vegas

Billy Mac picked up the phone to call his friend Pokey James in Vegas. He was a private investigator that Billy Mac had met at a Vegas convention two years ago, and this wasn't the first time he had asked Pokey to help him. A lot goes on in Las Vegas. Billy Mac had several clients who wanted their spouses spied upon in Sin City.

"Hello, How's my Golden Boy?" Pokey said as he answered the call.

"Yo! Pokey!" Billy Mac laughed. "If I weren't me, I'd get in line to be."

"You got somebody touching down out here?"

Billy Mac went through all the particulars, including flight arrival details, hotel reservations, and promised pictures and descriptions of Tank and Greg to be texted that evening.

"I will personally handle this. That way, you will have the best detective in Vegas covering for you." Pokey assured him.

"Invoice me by email, and I'll send payment to your PayPal account." Billy Mac said. "Thanks, this one is a little more important than most."

JoAnn beeped in while they were on the phone. After hanging up with Pokey, Billy Mac immediately called her back.

"Hey, I was on a business call," he apologized. "Got a lot going on"

"It's good to hear you're keeping busy." JoAnn began. "I hope you're planning on seeing your sweetheart tonight. There's somewhere I want you to take me."

"You bet your bippee, I am! I'll take you to the ends of the earth. Where are we going?"

"Well, my parents, they want us to come over for grilled burgers and hot dogs. Dad said if you came, he would perform his Denzel Washington impression for you."

Billy Mac chuckled. "Sounds like an exciting evening. I'd love to officially meet your parents. What time should I pick you up?"

"5:30 p.m. Very casual, I'm wearing shorts."

"Okay, see you soon."

Chapter 16

Meeting the Parents

Billy Mac wore khaki Bermuda shorts, dark blue and orange polo, a brown belt, and blue and orange Hoka trail shoes. JoAnn wore khaki shorts with a green, red, and blue Mickey and Minnie Mouse shirt and long red earrings with red sandals.

On the way, Billy Mac filled her in on his conversation with Missy and asked if it was okay to make her a silent partner, nothing official involving money or anything. He'd never ask for information about any of her patients. Making her a partner, he would be able to discuss everything with her and maintain his integrity.

JoAnn was very pleased about the arrangement.

Thank you, Lord, Billy Mac said to himself.

The Underwoods were like JoAnn, classy, and affable. He had been in social settings with them several times before, but this was more casual and important. This time he was meeting the parents" and understandably apprehensive.

Billy Mac's apprehension was for nothing. He immediately fell in love with JoAnn's parents and, in his humble opinion, just awesome!

JoAnn's father was around 65 and tall. When they got there, he immediately put him at ease, "Come on, Billy Mac. Let's go burn some red meat."

"Dad, what about Denzel? You promised, and at the risk of sounding petulant, we got to have that first!"

"Oh, well, of course, I did promise you."

Vanessa looked up to the sky and whispered, "Dear Lord, please let us live through this."

"Shhh… please." He turned around and left the room, then knocked on the wall.

"Come in," shouted JoAnn.

John entered. He was definitely in character, doing the little shrug Denzel does with his shoulders and chin to perfection. John then started the eye thing that Denzel did in The Equalizer. First, he cast his eyes toward Vanessa, then to Billy Mac, then to JoAnn. Then John spoke as Denzel. He looked at his watch and said, "Good evening, it is evening, isn't it? And evening is a good time to do what I gotta do." His mannerisms were perfect. "I guess you wanna know what I gotta do, and I'm gonna tell you what I gotta do. I gotta kick your ass. Do you know what I mean by kicking your ass?"

The dialogue continued for about twenty more seconds; John was excellent.

"JoAnn, you didn't tell me your father was better than I am!"

Billy Mac was now doing his Denzel. "I have to go back to work. I got work to do."

Everyone laughed, and the men went out and started the meat. The evening progressed nicely.

While they were seated and eating, Vanessa turned and spoke to Billy Mac. "Our little girl is so happy. I guess that is as understated as I can make it. And, if she's happy, then we're happy."

Billy Mac became very emotional. He felt a lump in his throat and fought back tears.

JoAnn noticed and went over to him, leaning her head against his head and put her arm around him, helping him regain his composure.

"I'm sure you can see how deliriously happy I am; we are! I still worry there might be problems with people accepting our relationship, you know, being interracial. It is still the South. I've told JoAnn more times than I can count how much I admire you guys; you've had so much to overcome. I can't guarantee she's gonna want to be with me forever, but while she'll have me, I promise to love and protect her with my own life.

"Anyone watching you two would get that message loud and clear!" Vanessa smiled.

"Just don't hurt my little girl." John said. "We preachers can pack a pretty punch! Only joking, Billy Mac, only joking."

JoAnn and Billy Mac stayed for dessert and said their goodbyes. The evening ended with hugs and well wishes from her parents.

What incredible people, thought Billy Mac.

"Your parents are almost too good to be true. I felt so welcome like they've known me for years."

"I'm blessed to have them as parents." JoAnn smiled at him. "I believe they liked you."

Billy Mac spent the night with JoAnn. Their lovemaking was tender and accentuated by a full moon shining through the bedroom window. It put a soft glow on everything it touched, especially JoAnn.

The next morning was Sunday, and they decided to attend church services. It was their first real outing in a public place since they'd begun to date. A few heads turned, and some people were staring. However, their looks alone would turn heads.

They chose to attend services at the Episcopal Church where JoAnn's father had been the pastor. After church, they went to lunch at Riverview Marina, known for its fresh seafood. Then, it was back to JoAnn's for a short nap. Billy Mac left to go home soon after they awoke. They both had some work to do to get a jump on Monday morning and needed a full night's sleep.

Chapter 17

Cleveland Ohio - David Dingler and Jeff Thomas

David Dingler was on his laptop, looking at an online website where LGBTQ meet. You could also research LGBTQ bars and clubs across the US, but he was looking in Riverview, Alabama. Several bloggers had recommended the Boardwalk and a bar called Partners. It was a place by the river where many from the LGBTQ community meet.

David knew he would have time on his own, at least forty-eight hours before he and Jeff went to the party. He wanted to have some fun and was getting sick and tired of Jeff. He knew Jeff didn't love him and that he was cheating on him with women. This trip was going to be their last rodeo, especially if he found someone new. Of course, he needed to find someone with money; why work when you don't have to?

It was Sunday evening. While David was online on the porn site, Jeff called Billy Mac.

"Well, hello, bud."

"Hey man, I got you a heads up." Jeff said. "We're flying into Atlanta and renting a car to drive the rest of the way. It's a week from Wednesday, the 29th. How about Thursday for lunch?

"Sure, I've penciled you in." Billy Mac replied.

"Good. Listen, give me your address. I need to hire you. This kid, Dingler, is running around on me big time!"

"It's not that I wouldn't take the job," Billy Mac began, "but it would cost you a lot less money to hire someone local. I would need to spend at least a week there and be charging you lodging and travel expenses in addition to my fee."

"No worries, money is no object. I don't mean to brag," Jeff hesitated then continued, "but I've made some pretty lucrative investments. I want you because I trust you. Don't forget to shoot me your address; I've got something to overnight you. See ya soon."

"All right, will do, see you soon."

# # # #

As soon as he hung up with Jeff, Billy Mac dialed JoAnn.

"Hello, I was just thinking about you."

"Nice to hear; I was afraid I might be interrupting your work."

"What? I'm having a little trouble hearing you. Did you say we're having a slumber party?"

"Yeah, that's what I said. Do you have slumber party pj's?"

"I'm afraid not, pj's are one piece of clothing I've never supported, but I do have something I think you'll like. What time does the party start?"

"Whenever you get here."

"Can't wait."

# # # #

Later that evening, JoAnn arrived with a sack full of groceries, wearing jeans and a striped tank top, sexy as ever.

"Whatcha got?" Billy Mac asked.

"I thought we'd make some tacos."

"Not only gorgeous but a mind reader as well! I was just thinking about tacos yesterday, how'd you know?"

While JoAnn was cooking and seasoning the ground beef, Billy Mac was chopping. He had an array of jalapenos, lettuce, tomatoes, and onions on his wooden board. They were two busy little homemakers.

"I know you've been reluctant to ask about my state of mind regarding the cancer possibility." JoAnn began. "So, I'll bring it up. I'm fine. I've spoken with God about it, and he has comforted me. My appointment is Wednesday in Birmingham at the Kirkland Clinic. Having you take me is a great comfort. Everything is going to be fine; I feel it down to my soul."

She gave him a big hug.

"Been doing a lot of praying myself." Billy Mac said. "Have you told your Mom and Dad?"

"No, so segue to whatever. Your turn."

Billy Mac gave her a bit of a scolding look.

"Jeff called me today. He wants me to come to Cleveland to do surveillance on his partner. I assured him it would be more prudent for him to hire someone local. He was very insistent, so I laid out what it would cost him. It's weird how he and Missy insist on using me. That seems hinky to me. Also, he wanted me and no one else; seems odd, the way he left things when he took off."

"So, what's your famous gut telling you?" JoAnn asked.

"It doesn't feel right. I want to trust him, but I'm finding it hard. Did I ever tell you he enjoyed torturing frogs when we were kids? I couldn't stomach being with him when he did it. He also liked to set fires in trash cans. He was a suspect in a fire when we were camping with the Boy Scouts. Someone set the cabin on fire. They never could prove it was him, but I don't have doubts. I don't even know why I was friends with him, but I was, and we were thick as thieves."

"My goodness!" Jo Ann exclaimed. "Do you know if he was a bedwetter? I know, weird question, just humor me."

"Yes! He spent the night at my house a lot, and he sometimes did wet the bed. A couple of other people said he did the same thing when he was sleeping over at their house." Billy Mac paused, then continued. "Eventually, he just stopped going to sleepovers. Why do you ask?"

"You got your phone handy?"

"I'll get it. It's in the den."

When he got back, JoAnn told him to Google the McDonald Triad.

He did as she requested and began to read out loud. "It says the triad links cruelty to animals, obsession with fire, and persistent bed-wetting past a certain age, to violent behaviors, particularly homicidal and sexually predatory behavior."

"That doesn't mean he's a serial killer or sexual predator," Jo Ann said, "but it does speak to his lack of honesty and flawed character. I would need extensive research on him, though, to make any kind of diagnosis."

"It's your area of expertise. After all, you fly all over the country, testifying at trials. I'm sure you'd be able to tell if he were telling the truth or not; you should come to lunch with me."

"Yes, I am an expert witness, but even experts disagree on evaluations of individuals. Just as a jury would disagree on an innocent or guilty verdict or a parole board may disagree on whether or not an inmate is suitable for release. Psychology is not an exact science, and by the way, you do not need me at lunch; you'll do fine on your own."

"All this talk made me hungry. Are you ready to eat some tacos?"

"Do you want me to get placemats for the dining room table?"

"Yes, the placemats are in the drawer over here."

The tacos were delicious. JoAnn had brought meat she purchased at Tank's Butcher Shop. After all, Tank's slogan was "A Cut Above."

Billy Mac didn't tell JoAnn that Tank kept him furnished with meat and other products from there. All the ingredients that Billy Mac chopped were fresh from Tank's shop. And the Taco shells were homemade at Tank's bakery.

They discussed Jeff briefly over dinner, then moved on to the party, which was only a couple of weeks away. JoAnn told him she had received reports that everything was going smoothly. But she had received another threatening email that said 'back out now, or you'll be sorry. The other volunteers reported that Emily was doing a fantastic job of decorating the Pitman. JoAnn purposely refrained from getting involved in overlooking the volunteer members. She didn't want to appear to be a straw boss or cause any distress. Everyone that volunteered was extraordinarily competent, and the party seemed to be right on schedule.

JoAnn was scooping Breyers Vanilla ice cream into a big bowl with Billy Mac written on it. She poured a generous amount of plain old Hershey's chocolate over it. She learned this was one of Billy Mac's favorites.

Billy Mac sat watching silently in anticipation, sporting a big grin on his face. Then he heard that little musical sound his phone makes when a text is coming through.

He looked down. The text was from Pokey. "The Eagle has landed and checked into the Bellagio. I'm already there and watching them like an old circling hawk looking for a rabbit. Will be in touch.... Pokey."

Billy Mac laughed and showed the text to JoAnn, "This is my friend in Vegas, spying on our locals."

"Funny text; he sounds like quite a character."

"He is and an outstanding detective. It'll be interesting to see what dirt he comes up with."

They cleaned up the dishes and journeyed to the couch in the den.

As they snuggled, JoAnn quizzed, "Who's in charge of the remote tonight?"

"You are dear, who else?"

"Ok, you asked for it, funny man. I'm going to choose one that was made more than a decade before you were born, and I'm going to sing."

And sing she did through that wonderful old movie, "Singing in the Rain". They did not make love that night; they were much too tired. Billy Mac held her in his arms as they snuggled, his new favorite activity. Feeling content, they quickly fell asleep.

Right before he drifted off, Billy Mac thought to himself, Thank you, God, I'm so happy! Please let her be okay Wednesday.

Chapter 18

The Kirkland Clinic, Birmingham, Alabama

At 7 am on the dot, JoAnn and Billy Mac pulled into the Kirkland Clinic. Billy Mac noted the Oncologist, Dr. Angelou, was Harvard trained and a stunning black woman. She saw patients at the clinic instead of UAB Hospital. The Kirkland Clinic had cutting edge diagnostic equipment and provided a more relaxed setting than the hospital. They had not waited long before they were called.

Dr. Angelou greeted them with a big smile. JoAnn immediately introduced Billy Mac.

She invited them to sit. "I have excellent news. You do not have cancer. We were able to remove the knot from your breast completely and saw nothing in your lymph nodes. The tumor we removed was benign."

Billy Mac sighed and raised his arms and exclaimed, "Thank you, Lord, Thank you!"

"I will want to see you every year for your exam and mammogram."

"Absolutely. You don't need to tell me twice. See you in a year!"

JoAnn and Billy Mac left the office elated. They were at peace during their sixty-minute ride home.

"Hey, Billy, what was your favorite action figure or baby doll you played with growing up?"

"Um, let me think. It's hard to remember all their names, hmmm, probably Wonder Woman, or are you referring to the live ones?"

JoAnn punched him on the arm.

"Ouch! That hurt, after all, you asked."

It was a playful mood for two relieved people, who were very much in love.

Billy Mac let JoAnn out at her house. She was going to give the news to her parents and needed to pick up her car.

Billy Mac felt like that should be a solo run for her.

Chapter 19

At the Underwood

John and Vanessa were watching a new Netflix drama when JoAnn arrived.

As JoAnn unveiled her story, her mom began to get that stern, authoritative expression only a former school principal can muster. It was the scary expression that stopped students dead in their tracks.

"Please don't give me that look. I'm sorry, I didn't tell you. I didn't want you to worry."

"Looks like you're going to be called to the principal's office."

Vanessa began to cry softly, and JoAnn jumped up and began hugging her. "Mama, it's okay, I'm fine. I didn't want you to worry."

Thirty minutes later, the drama had subsided. Vanessa went to the bathroom to freshen up.

"Dad, I made a mistake; I should've come to you guys when I got the original diagnosis."

"I don't know about that; your mother would have worried sick. You did what felt right to you. Believe it or not, there are many things I don't know for sure. I do know this, however," pointing to the bathroom, "You and that woman in there are just alike. Can you imagine how I've suffered?"

JoAnn didn't stay long and told her parents she had to get home and work. She needed to reschedule some appointments.

# # # #

Soon after dropping JoAnn off, Billy Mac's phone rang.

"Ok golden boy, I got the goods on your boys, at least one of them. That Hendricks fellow, I got all kinds of pics on him. My Lord, that man gets a lot of room service, and I have some great shots. 'Course you know the Bellagio wouldn't like that too much if they knew guest privacy, they get a bit testy. Anyway, that Hoss is quite the philanderer. Spent most of his time here shacked up with some pretty ladies and very little time at the Funeral Directors show.

On the flip side, his buddy worked his ass off in that booth, and when he wasn't there, he was eating or in his room. He and Hoss hosted one dinner together. I gather it was business. The only thing that boy would be guilty of is coming to Vegas and not having a good time. He didn't look happy to be here, but Sistern is clean."

"Thanks, man! What would I do without you?"

"Hire another private detective!"

"Not on your life! Matter of fact, I may be coming to Vegas with someone special. I thought we could get together."

"Sounds good to me, Golden Boy. Always your backside. See you!"

Chapter 20

The Sisterns'

Greg and Amanda were having breakfast for dinner. Greg had prepared one of Amanda's favorites, scrambled eggs with hard white cheddar, smokehouse bacon from Tank's butcher shop, buttered raisin toast, and fried apples. He always made her favorite when he wanted to talk about something important.

"Honey, what would you think of us selling out here and starting over, moving back to Texas?"

Amanda looked at him quizzically. "Have you been smoking loco weed you brought back from Vegas?"

"No, I'm serious. I think Hoss would buy the bank with the right offer and our interest in the funeral home."

"Where's this coming from? Our life is here, you know I love this house. We're making money hand over fist between the bank and funeral home interests. Compared to Alabama, with the mountains and waterfalls, Texas is bland. We're close to Atlanta and a day's drive to the Emerald Coast in Florida. Did you forget our plans to buy a house there?"

"No, but we can still do that and live in Texas. Frankly, I'm tired of both the banking and funeral business. After this last convention, I'm ready to be done. It's a pain in the ass! I'm uncomfortable with Hoss and the way he does business. I could always retire and paint. It's not like money is an issue. I love making money as much as the next guy, but we have enough."

"Greg, we're not moving to Texas, and we're absolutely not selling the bank or our interest in the funeral home. We make way too much money, and I like money. I don't mean to be dismissive of you. I want you to be happy, but what you're proposing is ridiculous.

Of course, there's a way you could retire and not give up our current income. We could trade places. I've got a good sense of both businesses and a brilliant head on my shoulders. I don't know what you mean about Hoss, as long as he makes us money, who cares if he's shady. I'd have him wrapped around my little finger and doing my bidding in no time."

"Are you serious? I'm not saying he's doing anything unethical or illegal, but are you sure you could handle him? He's not easy to work with, got a real bossy streak, even bosses around Booley! Sometimes I think I'm nothing more than a figurehead."

"I'm DEAD serious, excuse the pun. I'm quite sure Hoss respects you."

"The jury's out on that one, but now that I think about it, this may just work. I'll run it by Hoss. It wouldn't be right to switch places without a heads up. You make a good point about not giving up our business dealings; it's not like we have to. We'll discuss everything later on after I talk to Hoss, deal?"

"Deal." Amanda reached out and gave Greg a high five.

# # # #

Riverview Police Chief Booley Lancaster was leaving his office to get in his patrol car. He defied all notions of what a Chief of Police should look like. He was not an attractive man. Narrowed shoulders formed the top part of his upper torso sloping down to a pot belly in front and a drooping rear end that endeared him to the nickname "satchel ass" in high school. He wore an obvious toupee that sat atop a round, pudgy face with a double chin. His voice was high pitched, reminiscent of inhaling a helium balloon: all that, plus a personality void of humor.

No one could determine how he got to be the police chief. Many of the officers on the force did not like or respect him. It was a mystery how he got appointed police chief. Rumors were that Hoss filled the pockets of some local politicians to get him appointed. No one knows why but Booley kowtowed to Hoss at every turn.

Another rumor about Booley pertained to himself and Billy Mac. It was more than a rumor. There was bad blood between Booley and Billy Mac. Booley had fired him about ten years ago, where he would have counseled anyone else. At the time, Billy Mac was the best detective on the force by far, but he had a problem with alcohol. He did, in fact, technically drink on the job while working a case. He was in a bar, and Booley found out. It didn't make a difference that it was only a couple of drinks. Billy Mac expected disciplinary action, but not to lose his job. Booley disliked Billy Mac. It was apparent he was envious and jealous of him. Rather than write a counseling and mandatory AA, he fired him. Billy Mac learned later that it had been a set up to give Booley cause to fire him, but it was no secret in town they despised each other.

Booley drove his patrol car downtown to cruise by the Pitman, currently being decorated for the event. He wasn't a member of the POETS and never would be. He knew he wasn't well-liked. The only way he could attend the event was as a city official, and he planned to enjoy himself.

He left the Pitman and crossed the river to the East side of town where the bar, Partners, was located. There was an area of the boardwalk popular with the LGBTQ community. Booley was particularly interested in who was on the boardwalk, though he kept to himself. He had not officially come out, nor did he intend to. He thought he was keeping it under his hat and any rendezvous he had were always a couple of towns over.

He really should've known he couldn't keep the secret at work. His officers knew even though Booley was married, he preferred men, and his marriage was nothing more than an arrangement. A few years ago, an anonymous package arrived at his house that contained a tee-shirt. The card with it said, The Force is With You, and the tee-shirt said Our leader would prefer a Peter. Booley preferred to feign ignorance and didn't investigate who sent it. He didn't let it bother him, he may only be a puppet, but he was still the chief at the end of the day.

As Booley drove through the parking lot at Partners and around the Boardwalk, he received several waves from some of the regulars. He may be a puppet, but there were people in town who liked him. He then drove on home, anxious to see what his wife had prepared for dinner, and he was starving. He had married her because she did not speak much English, and he figured she would never find out about his sexual preference. Plus, she was one hell of a cook.

Chapter 21

Billy Mac, JoAnn, and Zora

JoAnn heard her phone ring and checked her caller ID. It was still early in the morning to be getting any business calls.

"Hello?"

"Right back at ya! Are you going to that women's business thing?"

"Yes, the Women's Business Association wants me to join, apparently not asking me to join was an embarrassing oversight on their part, or so their president said. I did notice there aren't many minorities in the group. My best guess is Zora got that ball rolling. By the way, she called and wants to treat you and me to lunch at Red Lobster before the association meeting at 5. The meeting shouldn't last more than a couple of hours, but I've got important plans, and I'm not letting this get in the way."

"So, exactly what are your plans for later that evening?"

"To leave shortly after 6 o'clock and spend the night at my boyfriend's house, of course. Oh, I almost forget to tell you, Zora wants you to have lunch with us."

"Why? I'm not a prospect for the Women's Business Association, am I? Though I would make a great woman."

"No, but her exact words were, and I quote, "Bring that boyfriend of yours with you. Honey, Emily tells me he is beyond handsome, a hunk, and I've a mind to have lunch with a handsome hunk of a man."

"Lawdy Mercy, that pumped my ego up! It's a great plan, except for lunch; I'm not sure I'm comfortable being someone's eye candy."

"Oh, you're coming. Zora can stare all she wants."

"Alright, then, what time do I pick you up?"

"No need, Zora's already planning to pick me up. Just meet us there at noon."

"Ten-four, see you there. Bye."

Billy Mac arrived first. Red Lobster had reserved a table in the back, away from other diners. Zora must have some pull; Red Lobster is not known for accommodating reservations.

The hostess led Billy Mac to the table where he sat facing the door so he could see the girls when they came in. It was a chilly April morning, one of those they called Blackberry winters in the South. It was perfect weather for his favorite white cashmere V-neck sweater and black silk tee-shirt. Khaki pants, his favorite socks, white polka dots outlined in orange, and black penny loafers. He still had thick, shiny, blonde hair that hadn't been touched with grey like so many of his peers.

The waitress brought Billy Mac unsweetened tea with extra lemon. As he was squeezing the lemon into the tea, the girls arrived. JoAnn had on beige pants with a white low-cut top, a yellow scarf, beige high heels, with a matching pleated purse. All he could think about was how sexy she looked.

Zora was wearing a bright pink jacket over a black linen blouse and black pants and carried a simple black handbag. She was an elegant woman.

Billy Mac rose from his seat, gave JoAnn a peck on the cheek, and extended his hand toward Zora.

"So nice to meet you, Billy Mac."

She took his hand while secretly thinking about how easily he could get her juices flowing.

"Likewise. Wow, both of you look amazing."

Both women thanked him.

"So, have the women decided to allow men into the WBA?

"Nope, but men are welcome tonight as long as a member invites them. And, officially tonight, JoAnn will be a member."

"Oh, I didn't know I could invite someone! You want to go with me, Billy?"

"Absolutely, is what I'm wearing acceptable, or is the dress code more formal?"

"No, you're dressed perfectly; after all, suits and ties are almost nonexistent these days."

"That's what I think. I have hardly any suits but lots of clothes. JoAnn has accused me of being a clothes hound. She said I have more clothes than she does."

"His closet looks like mine, lots of pants, shirts, shoes, and coordinating belts. And a few cowboy hats and boots."

"Ah, a well-dressed gentleman for sure. I must admit I have an ulterior motive in inviting you to lunch. I want to hire you to investigate one of my employees. Perhaps we can meet in my office, first thing in the morning?"

"No need to wait until tomorrow. We can talk business over lunch. I've used JoAnn's expertise as a consultant so often that it just made sense to make her a partner so we can talk freely in front of her."

"Wonderful, and congratulations on the partnership. She's a wonderful friend to have on your side."

"What do you need, Zora?"

"Well, talking about partnerships, I must confide I have a stake in Moyer Cutler Funeral Home in addition to my funeral home. JoAnn, I didn't mention it the last time we met. It's not particularly relevant to my story and not something I advertise. After all, I began my business for the black community. Moyer Cutler had taken advantage of them for years. Of course, my goal is to even the field, and I've had some success.

But you know how it is around here; a person's perception could destroy years of work. Anyway, I'm not doing anything illegal, unless making money is!"

"No problem, no one will ever find out from me or Billy!"

"Do you know a gentleman named Cortez Cortez?"

"Yes, I do. Cortez works part-time with a good buddy of mine, Tank, the local butcher. Tank says there's no one better with a knife than Cortez; he'd make a great butcher."

"Oh my, this makes what I'm hiring you for a bit awkward, but I think he may be stealing from Moyer Cutler and me. I hear he's been using a fence to move the stolen property, but I have no proof one way or the other. Plus, he has a prior history of drug abuse. I need a trained investigator to follow him and report back to me. Of course, I'm hoping to be proven wrong."

"I'm not trying to be ignorant, but what would one steal from a funeral home?"

"Good question, Billy Mac. For one thing, embalming fluid, which we're missing inventory on and one of our embalming machines. Did you know you can dip any type of cigarette into embalming fluid, and it produces a hallucinogenic or a happy high? It's the new thing with some of the kids. We think he may be trafficking this on the side.

Also, a few clients had items stolen from their cars while here during visitation hours or funerals of a loved one. And this is the most bizarre; we are also short two caskets. Before you ask, Cortez does most of his work at Moyer Cutler but also does some embalming for us."

Cortez's prior history of drug abuse was not new to Billy Mac; they often attended the same AA meetings. But that was a decade ago; of course, he didn't know Cortez well, so his sobriety could be in question.

"I need to be honest; we're working a couple of cases right now, and I'm not able to take this on immediately. Can it wait a week or so?"

"Yes, that's not a problem. I don't want to hire someone second rate. You're highly recommended."

"I'll let you know in the next few days when I'll be able to start."

"Good, I'll wait to hear from you then.

The rest of the luncheon was social. JoAnn made sure Zora was invited to the Friends Faceoff. Then everyone said, see you tonight, goodbye.

# # # #

A couple of hours after lunch, Billy Mac and JoAnn were on their way to the Chamber of Commerce building for cocktail hour.

"I suspect you don't feel comfortable with the Cortez situation," said JoAnn.

"Nope, I'm not sure why, but it's all a bit hinky. First, Missy hires me to follow Hoss, paid ahead and upfront. Number two, Zora wants me to surveil Cortez, who works for Hoss, and she's paying ahead. Of course, I could just tell her that I'm already surveilling Hoss, and I could kill two birds with one stone, save her a bundle. Of course, that's not ethical."

JoAnn threw her head back and laughed as she went into the old Oliver Hardy, "Well, here's another nice mess you've gotten me into."

"Hey, any more emails? I've been meaning to ask you."

"No, not since I put you on the case!"

They both started laughing convulsively, non-stop, the kind that comes from pent up emotion.

The party was a social test for JoAnn and Billy Mac, bigotry was not dead yet, and interracial couples weren't running rampant in their town. Plus, this was only the second time they went as a couple to a large social gathering. Being the subject of the gossip girls was not something either of them particularly wanted.

They had no reason to be apprehensive. It turned out that a few people they knew told them it was about time. There would always be bigotry in small towns, but for the most part, their small slice of the South was a bit more progressive.

"That wasn't so bad. I was expecting to be put to sleep on my feet!"

"You do know how to phrase things. I think we gave the gossip girls enough to keep them busy for months! I dare say, they all looked a bit envious. I had the best looking guy there or any guy for that matter!"

After that, they talked shop. Billy Mac told JoAnn about seeing Cortez at a few of his AA meetings.

"There were always a few NA folks at our meetings. Guess we had better coffee and donuts! Kidding aside, I don't see Cortez stealing or pushing drugs. I'm sure Tank would have mentioned if he thought there was a problem, but seeing as how we're gonna take the job, might as well get started."

He dialed, and Tank answered on the first ring, "Hey Bud, what's going on?"

"JoAnn and I are on our way home from that women's cocktail party at the Chamber. Say hi to JoAnn. You're on speaker."

"Hello, beautiful one."

"Hey there, Billy Mac fixed me some of that smokehouse bacon of yours recently, yummy, yummy."

"Well, that's why we say we are a cut above; glad you enjoyed it."

"Tank, does Cortez still work for you on occasion?"

"He does, matter of fact, something kind of strange happened recently. He called me, wanted to meet at the shop and talk. Naturally, I was curious. Turns out, he wants to work for me full time, said he wanted to quit working at the funeral home. He seemed real nervous. Between you and me, I'd love to have him. I had to tell him that I can't afford to pay him enough to live on. It didn't bother him. I told him I'd think on it."

"Listen, bud; we need to keep this conversation down-home. It never happened. I don't want Cortez to know I'm asking questions about him but, do you think he'd steal?"

"Uh, Uh, No Way! He has had all kinds of opportunities to steal from me, and he hasn't. Far as I'm concerned, he's a good man!"

"You're the best Tank, don't ever let anybody tell you otherwise, over and out."

"Wait, who wouldn't find me great? Y'all be safe, talk soon."

After hanging up, the two continued their discussion.

"Well, what did you think of Zora?"

"My mind says, great resume. My gut says something seems off. I just can't put my finger on what it is."

"Yeah, kinda what I've been thinking. Well, my job is to get all this off your mind tonight. Like Liam Neeson said, 'I've got a special set of skills, just a little different than his. I plan to implement them," as she gently stroked the palm of his hand with her index finger.

The night was blissful, and JoAnn did indeed get everything off his mind. The night was torrid with ardent, passionate lovemaking and some good conversation thrown in.

The next morning JoAnn was poaching eggs and had hot sausage cooking slowly in the frying pan, Jewish rye in the toaster, and coffee brewing. As an after-thought, she decided to add a few cheese grits. She figured Billy Mac might be extra hungry.

She decided to go with a lighter breakfast. She put an apple, blueberries, non-fat yogurt, whey protein, skim milk, and a little ice into the blender, set it on smoothie, and watched it whir.

"Hey, Billy, can you pour the coffee while I serve your plate?"

"No problem, where's your plate, or is it your plan to fatten me up?"

"Ha, ha, funny. I don't usually eat a big breakfast; I just knew you did."

"I think I have an answer to the Zora dilemma I'm feeling. I know she was very specific regarding only wanting me. My friend Pokey, who lives in Vegas, is a top-notch private eye. He and I have worked together before. He sends me business; I send him a lot of business. Anyway, he's always wanted to visit. I've toyed with the idea of inviting him to the party. What if we subcontracted the job to him? We can't tell Zora we have a conflict of interest regarding Hoss, but could say I'm uncomfortable as Cortez is a friend."

"And you really think Pokey would come?"

"I think he would love to come."

"Do it! If he can come, we'll talk to Zora, tell her we are subcontracting due to a conflict of interest."

Billy Mac made the call to Pokey. Just as he figured, Pokey was delighted to come to Riverview and could always use the work. He said he could arrive early next week to start surveillance.

For business reasons, Billy Mac agreed that Pokey needed to stay in a motel, not with Billy Mac, to avoid tongues wagging. It was always better not to mix business with pleasure. Billy Mac said he would call him as soon as he finalized with Zora.

JoAnn put in a call to Zora. Billy Mac explained his relationship with Cortez and that he felt unethical taking the job. He lauded Pokey with praise, telling Zora next to himself, there was no better private detective.

Zora agreed and said she would send a $10,000 advance over by messenger first thing. It seemed quite a large sum. Billy Mac said that after Pokey's time and expenses were calculated, whatever was left would be returned to her; it was very generous.

"We'll see about returning even a portion of the fee, but this arrangement should work fine. I just hope Cortez really has done nothing wrong; I do like him."

"I've been a detective for twenty-five years, and since the very beginning, I've always followed my gut. Of course, my gut doesn't always reconcile with the evidence. I'm hoping the same thing, though, that he's innocent."

Chapter 22

The Final Planning Meeting

The final POETS meeting at the Warehouse had begun. One week from tomorrow was the big event. All eighteen POETS members were present, eager to hear the latest developments.

JoAnn spoke, "How much better could this be? All of our members are in attendance today; I won't drag this out. Let's get started. Missy, how many have responded so far?"

"About 480, and we've collected about $12,000. We only have room for 70 more. I think everyone we've invited is coming."

JoAnn continued to ask the other volunteers for updates, and all was going well.

After a couple of questions from the floor, the meeting ended, and the camaraderie began. An hour and a half later, the crowd had dispersed.

Billy Mac and JoAnn spent the rest of the weekend relaxing, with a little exercise and a lot of Netflix, especially Longmire.

"We could sure use Longmire next week. That's when crunch time begins. Pokey will be here Monday to start surveilling Cortez. I'm meeting with Jeff Thursday and have follow-up surveillance to do on Hoss. What's the expression, too many irons in the fire?"

"I wouldn't use that one. That's more of a wintery saying. I would just stick with 'shit fire and save the matches'."

"When was the last time you had a proper ass-whupping?"

JoAnn jumped him. Nothing like a little love making to interrupt Longmire.

# # # #

"Golden Boy, Pokey's here."

"Are you at the Hampton?"

"Yep, pretty nice quarters."

"Good, I'll come by and pick you up soon. JoAnn is cooking for us tonight at her house."

"Can't wait, Golden Boy."

Billy Mac picked Pokey up at the Hampton. He was holding a dozen yellow roses.

"Oh, you shouldn't have."

"For your lady."

"She'll love them."

On the way, the two friends caught up. Pokey told him he had a girlfriend, someone he was serious about. The ride went fast, and before they knew it, they had arrived at their destination.

When JoAnn opened the door, Pokey bowed with a flourish and presented the flowers to her.

"Oh, Pokey, I love yellow roses! Come over here for a hug. It's nice to finally meet you. Billy Mac thinks the world of you. Matter of fact, you must walk on water."

"No, just puddles!"

JoAnn had baked Lasagna, extra cheesy, with imported cheeses. She was complimenting the meal with traditional garlic bread and fresh garden salad with Caesar dressing.

But first, the cocktail hour.

JoAnn's bar was well stocked, and Billy Mac took the order. Pokey chose the Chivas Regal, and Billy Mac gave him a very generous pour over ice. Pokey had no trouble putting away the booze, and Billy Mac knew it.

Before Billy Mac had served the drinks, JoAnn, a seasoned interrogator, was already pulling out of Pokey his life story; and it was fascinating.

"Momma died when I was twelve. My poppa was a professional gambler. We moved to Vegas so he could be close to the action. We packed up and left Hapeville, Georgia, which is just south of Atlanta. My father worked at the Ford plant there, but gambling was his passion. And, he was damn good at it, especially betting on football. He was also a bookie. I guess he paid the law off as long as he could; then, the political climate changed. The new regime began to put pressure on the law, so we moved.

He and I bonded pretty thick after my Momma passed. He got tight with some of the Vegas oddsmakers, even asked if he could audition for a job. One of them said, 'We don't hold auditions. This isn't a talent show.'

Poppa told him that was precisely what it was; he was going to show them his talent and how to increase their earning power. What he did was pick 100 football games against the spread for a season. He got seventy-five right. That's unheard of; Poppa was great in figuring what the spread would be.

To put that into perspective, if you bet $1,000, or a dime a game, as we call it, and picked 75 right, that's $75,000. You lose $27,500. So, you are still up $47,500. Do you understand why you lose $27,500, not $25,000?"

"Of course, Pokey, my dear, it's the juice money!"

"This woman is sharp, Billy Mac."

"You can't get much by her."

Pokey continued, "I started hanging out with my Poppa as often as I could. I just couldn't go into the casinos and gamble with him until I was twenty-one. Still, even in high school, I took after him, ran my own booking operation, and made a lot of money. Of course, as a gambler, security technology was intriguing. Eventually, it lured me in, and the rest is history. I've built one of the largest security agencies in the country.

I took a particular liking to this guy here. I've tried to hire him several times over the last ten years, just can't get him to Vegas! Maybe you can. You and Golden Boy, as I like to call him, should come on out to Vegas. I'll see y'all make plenty of money, see a lot of shows, plus you can meet my woman, Susan. It's a plain name, but nothing plain about her. This is a standing, whenever you want to come, invitation."

"We'll be sure to take you up on your offer soon."

After dinner, Billy Mac drove Pokey back to the hotel and went home to prepare for tomorrow's lunch mentally.

# # # #

Billy Mac worked hard at not dreading anything, but he was only human and was dreading the lunch date with Jeff. He knew he needed just to let it flow and relax. After all, the man had just sent him a $10,000 check. But it was Jeff, and Jeff had caused him nothing but trouble.

Another thing bothering him was why would three people within the past few weeks have given Logan Investigative Services $10,000 and have no connection themselves that he could think of beyond Missy and Jeff's previous relationship

As Billy Mac entered the Chili Parlor, he saw Jeff waving his hands from the back of the restaurant. They did the "big man hug, haven't seen you in a while" and then sat down.

"Billy Mac, you don't look a damn bit different."

"You haven't changed either, except for that salt and pepper look you're sporting."

"Oh, I try to stay in shape, go to the gym, eat healthy, and I don't smoke or drink, not even those expensive cigars. I do gamble, though. It's better than working."

"Funny, that's what they said at the steel plant."

"I know, I just up and left, no notice, and after you recommended me for the job. I hope it didn't cause you any trouble. I'm genuinely sorry. I'm here to beg your forgiveness and make amends with anyone else I caused hurt."

"You probably know I got Missy pregnant in high school. Turns out a daughter lives here, ironic isn't it?"

"Everyone knew you got Missy pregnant, but Missy only recently told me the baby was a girl and lives here."

"Did she tell you we're planning on telling her who we are after the party?"

"Missy did mention something about it, but not exactly when."

"I'm the one who wanted to wait until after the party, you know, in case there's drama. That's why David and I are staying through Monday night. We've got an early morning flight back to Atlanta on Tuesday. I'm considering sending him home after the party, so I don't have to deal with him and this whole parenting mess."

"Listen, man, I'm not tryin' to be a jerk, but you, gay? Especially with our upbringing, you know, church every Sunday. Don't get me wrong, I respect your choice, but never saw that coming."

Jeff smiled, "Dude, I'm not gay, I'm what ya call bisexual. Anyway, that's not important. David is after my money, I'm sure of it and have proof he's stealing from me. I had cameras installed in our apartment, behind Aunt Sophie's home, but the footage was mysteriously erased. Do you remember Aunt Sophie and Uncle William? They visited once. I think you came over and met them.

"I remember, he was an executive with General Electric and was in real estate, too, right?"

"That's right! Uncle William left me a million dollars in his will. Enough reminiscing, back to David, I think he's hired someone to kill me. Right after I took out a $100,000 life insurance policy on myself and made him my beneficiary, someone's been following me."

"Then why bring him?"

"It's obvious. I don't want David to become suspicious that I know anything before I've got proof. Plus, you know the saying, keep your friends close and your enemies closer. So, will you take the job?"

"Yeah, our past is under the bridge far as I'm concerned. Just give me a start date."

"What about Thursday? That'll give us time to settle back in."

"Sounds good. I don't foresee a conflict. I'll call you when I get into town. Should I use the number you gave me?"

"No, I'll get a burner and get the number to you, and thanks."

"No problem, just watch out for yourself. If you're right about David, you're not safe anywhere. Call if you need me before the party."

"I'll stay vigilant; see you Saturday."

# # # #

While Jeff was having lunch with Billy Mac, David was in Partners across the river. He was quizzing the bartender about some of the locals.

"This is a groovy bar if I can use one of those ancient words from a few decades ago."

"It's respectable," said Tyrone. "When I bought the place, it was a real dive. I classed it up, changed the name from the Cover-Up to

Partners, and the rest is history. Anyway, cover-up implies not being yourself. Polonius said it best: This above all; to thine own self be true, and it must follow as the night the day. Thou canst not then be false to any man."

"You're a classy man Tyrone, who owns a classy bar."

David continued the conversation with Tyrone telling him why he's in town and who he's with.

"I know all about Jeff. He's a legend, at least according to gossip. I never met him myself."

"I'll tell you something your gossip can't. He's a miserable man; I'm pretty sure he's a cheat too. I'm looking to end our relationship and find someone new. And have some fun in-between."

"With your looks, you'll have no trouble. The locals are going to love you. Hang out and have a few drinks, around 10 o'clock things begin to pick up. I guarantee there'll be several folks interested in you."

"Maybe. Hey, question, on my way into the bar, this guy pulled up, wanted to give me his number. He's an older unattractive man driving a white Dodge Ram truck. Told me to call if I was interested and then drove off. Showed me a wad of cash; the entire conversation lasted like a minute. Could he be a local pervert?"

"Don't know of any, probably just hoping you'd give him the time of day. Just watch out. You never know, even in a small town."

David took Tyrone up on the suggestion and hung around. He introduced himself to some locals and had a few drinks. He was having a good time but had another plan in mind.

He walked outside and made a phone call. Thirty minutes later, he was at Booley's house. He had left his car in the Walmart parking lot, where Booley had insisted on picking him up and spent the night.

Billy Mac was glad he started surveillance early. He had several perfect pictures of David and Booley, including David getting the paper at 6 in the morning, off the front porch, not even the decency to wear a robe.

Chapter 23

Billy Mac Warns Jeff Thomas

Billy Mac dialed Jeff's number, he answered on the second ring.

"Hello."

"Can you talk? If so, say, Hi, buddy. If not, just say, I enjoyed it too."

"Hi Buddy, David's out trolling, I think."

"Good, I thought I better start early. I started watching him."

"What happened?"

"He started at Partners, and met up with Booley Lancaster, spent the night at his house. Booley's the police chief now."

"Shit! Booley is the Police Chief?"

"Really? I give you all that, and your reaction is to Booley being the chief?"

"Just a shock, that's all, never did think he'd amount to a hill of beans in high school. He's never liked me. Of course, I did bully him back then, which puts him on the long list of folks I need to talk to. I'll be watching my backside."

"I figured as much. After what you told me the other day, I thought I'd start the job early, glad I did."

"I'm still not overly worried anything will happen to me while we're, but I certainly don't want to land in jail, know what I mean?"

"So, you still feel fairly safe?"

"Yes, and no, I'm sure I'm in danger, but fairly positive, David won't try anything himself. He's gutless. He'll wait 'till we're back in

Cleveland for his henchman. Anyway, you ready for the party? It's going to be some shindig. We can meet Sunday to talk business."

"Sunday then, if you do need me, I'm a phone call away, literally, bye."

# # # #

Later that same day:

It had been a risk bringing that boy to his house, but well worth every minute. His wife was away visiting family, and his house was on five acres, but you never know. That's why he met him at Walmart a couple of towns away.

Booley called David's number, nothing but voicemail; he didn't bother to leave a message. David told him not to leave any messages. That boy better call back, thought Booley. I gave him a lot of money to keep his mouth shut about me, and he promised me another night before he went back to Cleveland.

Chapter 24

Saturday Morning

Billy Mac was getting ready to call JoAnn when the phone rang. He answered the call. It was Missy.

"Hi, Billy Mac. I'm so sorry to call. I know it's the day of the party, so I'll be brief. Did you hear from Jeff?"

"Yes. We had lunch Thursday, and I talked to him on the phone yesterday morning. He told me y'all were going to tell Amanda your news on Sunday."

There was silence on the other end of the line.

"He was supposed to call me last night, and I haven't heard from him. I was worried he skipped town again."

"Well, he's never been the most dependable person in the world. Always been on what I like to call Jeff time."

"Yeah, I guess you're right. Remember, one dance tonight."

"I haven't forgotten. See you tonight."

Billy Mac thought about calling Jeff but didn't see any reason to worry. He was probably avoiding Missy. He called JoAnn instead.

"How's my lovely sweetheart?"

"Good and looking forward to this evening."

"Me too. Listen, I told Greg I'd meet him at the theater at 4 o'clock sharp."

"Okay, I'll be ready at 3:30. That'll give us plenty of time."

"Plenty of time? I guess romance is dead!"

"Very funny. I'll see you soon.

# # # #

The Big Event

It was a beautiful sunny day, complete with a gentle breeze fanning the air with anticipation and electrifying excitement. It was akin to a sporting event like the Alabama vs. Auburn game or a heavyweight championship fight. It was still early, and the only sound was the steady drone of the city's only street sweeper as the sizable circular brush cleaned the dirt from along the curbs of Broad Street.

Soon downtown would be bustling with activity as Emily, and the other volunteers put the finishing touches to the Pitman Theater's interior.

Billy Mac and JoAnn entered the theater precisely at 4 o'clock and couldn't believe how remarkable the room looked. Primary colors graced every table, right down to the coordinating flower arrangements serving as centerpieces.

Just about every inch of wall space was covered with enlarged profile pictures of each POETS member. One wall was dedicated to each member's senior portrait arranged around the three high schools entitled How it All Started.

While Billy Mac began scanning the room for Greg, JoAnn spotted Emily.

"Emily, this is absolutely gorgeous. I'm speechless, totally blown away by your creativity."

"Thank you! Decorating for the event has been great therapy, retirement sucks! I didn't realize how much I miss my interior design business. I was afraid I had lost my creative spark."

"You obviously didn't. I agree with JoAnn; you've done a great job."

"Y'all are too kind! Billy Mac, I see you're carrying a rather large suit bag. There isn't a body in there, I hope?"

"Well, kinda, sorta, just a small surprise, a visual aid for the program before the real partying starts. Speaking of which, I need to find Greg so we can do a run-through and sound check, etc., make sure he's feeling at ease."

"Okay, go, do your thing!"

"I don't have time for that right now, got an MC job."

JoAnn swatted at him as he turned away. Both women were laughing.

Billy Mac spotted Greg in the wings as he climbed onto the stage. Greg was pacing back and forth, muttering to himself.

"You look so relaxed, Billy Mac. I wish I were half as relaxed as you look. I forgot the cue cards, and I've been trying to work out what I'm going to say. I did remember my flask of liquid calm, double malt scotch. I need something to calm my mind, so I don't make a fool of myself."

"Greg, you'll be fine. Stop all your fretting. You'll forget all about your nerves once you say your first word. By the way, have you seen or heard from Tank? I guess he's waiting until the last minute to bring in the food."

"No, but I talked with Bobby Jean in the parking lot. She said he'd be here by 5:30. She was busy giving last-minute instructions to the kids that volunteered to valet park. You should see the size of the flashlights she gave them. Just one would light the entire parking lot!"

Tank had arrived while they were talking. He had his crew setting the food up buffet style on two long tables across from the stage. Tank was personally seeing that the beer, wine, and soda table was set up and ready to go.

Before long, the party vibe filled the theater. Guests began arriving, and happy confusion ensued as they searched for their tables, filled plates, and secured drinks.

At precisely 7 o'clock, the song "Celebration" echoed through the acoustically friendly speakers of the renovated theater.

A crowd of around five hundred was in the building. The party was in full bloom, and the human interaction was fast and furious.

Billy Mac entered downstage left, carrying a life-size cardboard cutout. As soon as he stepped fully onstage, the DJ cut off the music.

He could tell the audience was full of anticipation by the whispers. As soon as he was in front of the microphone, Billy Mac turned the cutout around. It was none other than the King of Social Media. There was much cheering, laughing, and clapping.

Before beginning his speech, Billy Mac put his arm around the cutout of the social media pioneer. "Hey, everyone, welcome. I'm Billy Mac Logan, and this is my friend. He's a bit stiff, so I need y'all to loosen him up. Are y'all ready to celebrate?" He turned his ear to the audience with his hand cupped behind it.

The audience shouted back, "Yeah!"

Billy Mac repeated the same gesture and said, "I can't hear you?"

The audience shouted back louder, "Yeah!!!"

"All right, everybody, welcome to Friends Faceoff. We want you to enjoy an evening full of fun and friendships, especially meeting new friends! Before I hand you over to the man of the hour, let's give a round of applause to Emily Watts, the creative genius behind the decorations. This place looks better than Carnegie Hall or a New York Opera House. Thank you, Emily. And right over there is my all-time best bud Tank Wilson, butcher extraordinaire. Can y'all believe how good this food is? Some other folks deserving your applause are Missy Hendricks, invitations, Bobbie Jean White Parking, and the lady in red, JoAnn Underwood. She is the brainchild of this whole idea. Let's give everyone who helped pull this party together a big hand!"

I'd like to introduce you now to the owner and CEO of Riverview Bank and the party's generous benefactor, Mr. Gregory Sistern."

There was applause from the audience as Greg entered downstage, right across from Billy Mac, and stopped at the microphone put in place for him.

"Welcome! Can I have a round of applause for this guy over here? I want to thank you all for coming and sharing your joy, memories, and laughter with us. To show just how much Riverview Bank is giving back. That is your money! Watch your mail for a refund over the next couple of weeks!"

The room was filled with thunderous applause from the audience and a few cat whistles as well. Greg was busy waving at the crowd and signaling for the room to settle.

At first, the applause covered the noise, but not for long. It sounded as if a giant locomotive was screeching to a halt right before crashing into the building. A man's body was suspended by a thick wire cable tied around the ankle swinging back and forth like a pendulum from the beams above.

It didn't take long for stunned silence to become shrieks of terror from the crowd. Loud gasps and screams resounded throughout the building. Chaos was about to ensue as people wildly began running to the closest exit.

Billy Mac, out of instinct, headed toward the body, but once he realized it was indeed the lifeless body of a man, quickly recovered and sprinted to the mike in an effort to calm the crowd and prevent further tragedy.

Once the Sheriff took over crowd control, Billy Mac went to get a better look at the body. The victim's shirt hung over his face exposing a bare torso and what looked like an appendix scar. He didn't have time to take a close look at the victim's face, but the scar told him all he needed to know in his mind. Hanging from a beam above was the dead body of Jeffrey Thomas.

"Please, everyone, take your seats and remain calm! Are Sheriff Langston and Chief Lancaster here?"

As he spoke, Billy Mac could see the Sheriff striding toward the stage with two deputies at his side.

When Sheriff Langston got to the microphone, he spoke calmly. "Folks, please, calm down. I realize how upsetting this situation is, but right now, our top priority is your safety. My deputies will direct you to the exits in an orderly fashion. I'm sure you will want to let the deputies know what you saw tonight, but it is of the utmost importance for us to see you safely out of the building and secure the scene. If your statement is required, we will contact you in due time. Thank you for your cooperation."

Sheriff Langston was a guest but had arranged for members of his department to work security in the unlikely event of trouble. More than one of the POETS members had received threatening emails about the party, and he believed in taking precautions.

Once the crowd was under control, Sheriff Langston looked around for Booley. He had expected him to show his face at this point. He placed a call to the police department as per protocol. Not even ten minutes later, Booley arrived with two officers in tow. He had initially planned on getting to the party around 8 o'clock. He wasn't entirely comfortable at parties.

At this point, Billy Mac, the Sheriff, and the Riverview Police Officers had already cordoned off the crime scene with yellow tape. No one had touched the body.

As soon as he arrived, Booley promptly ordered Billy Mac off the stage, stating that civilians weren't allowed inside crime scene perimeters.

Billy Mac just nodded and left the stage; he didn't want a confrontation with Booley. It wasn't worth the aggravation. On the way down the steps, he glanced over and saw Hoss looking at the body and talking to Booley. Strange that Booley hadn't chased Hoss off. He looked for Greg and saw he was busy being interviewed and figured he'd catch up with him later.

Billy Mac decided to call and touch base with JoAnn.

"Are you all right, Billy? I'm out here in the parking lot with Missy and Pokey."

"I'm good. Are you okay?"

"I'm fine, don't worry. The crowd is lingering outside, though. We could use some law enforcement out here to move people along."

"I know we could use a new police chief, he ordered me off the stage before his feet barely touched it, but I'm not leaving the building until I know more. Just stay close to Pokey until I can get to you. The crowd should start dispersing soon. People are just shook up."

"Well, Missy is badly shaken, so Pokey and I plan to stay with her until Hoss comes out. Hey, do you think it'd be a good idea, never mind, not a good idea?"

"What were you going to say?"

"Well, there are a couple of bars within walking distance, and I thought it might be a good idea to let people know where they are, give them someplace other than this dark parking lot to gossip."

"Actually JoAnn, it's a good idea. Most folks aren't going to want to go home after what they've just witnessed. Keep me posted on your whereabouts."

After Billy Mac hung up, the phone rang again; it was JoAnn.

"In the aftermath and confusion, I forgot to get clarification. Word is Jeff Thomas is the victim. Can you confirm?"

"Well, if I was a betting man, which I'm not, but if I was, I'd bet everything I had that it was Jeff. I didn't get a real good look at the face. It looked like him, but Jeff had his appendix out in high school, and I know I saw a scar. In my mind, it's him. Plus, he told me he was in danger but didn't think anything would happen until he was back home. I have no idea yet how they got him up there or triggered his release, but it had to have happened sometime yesterday. He had a lot of enemies, and I'm wondering if those emails are in some way connected. Hey, you sure you're okay, JoAnn?"

"Don't worry about me, I'm fine. But stay with me tonight."

"No problem, you don't even need to ask. I'm not about to leave you alone until I'm sure this is only about Jeff. I'll talk with you later. Tell Pokey what I'm doing."

Greg saw Billy Mac as soon as he was off the stage. "That's a hell of a way to get my talk interrupted."

"Did anyone identify the body?"

"Jeff Thomas," said Greg "Hoss and Booley both said there wasn't a doubt."

"Are you okay? You seem to be."

"A little shaken, it's not every day a dead body falls out of the sky and interrupts a great speech."

"You picked a hell of a way to get upstaged. Have you talked to Amanda? How is she?"

"Seems to be fine. Nothing much affects that woman, nerves of steel. She texted me a couple of times. I think she's with Missy and JoAnn."

"What about Hoss? I saw him poking around."

"Cool as a cucumber. He wants to get the body down and get it to the funeral home; he'd deemed it a suicide, no need for an investigation. The Sheriff wants a little more time to figure out how the body was released from up there and investigate, but it's Booley's jurisdiction, and Hoss runs the show."

"Any idea where it was released from? What was supporting it?"

"Not sure. There is a big steel beam, I think."

"Hey, I told you to leave Billy Mac," interrupted Booley. "Greg's been interviewed and has given us all the details we need, and you are not needed."

"Trying to help Booley. I'm a private detective. It's in my blood, and I may have some additional information, especially if it's a murder case. And it sure looks that way to me."

"Don't know what we'd do without your expertise. Go home, let me and my officers do our job. Goodbye, for now."

Billy Mac turned and walked toward the front door of the theater, muttering under his breath, that son-of-a-bitch has still got it in for me. I'll give him something to think about soon enough.

Chapter 25

Billy Mac, JoAnn, Pokey, and Tank

Billy Mac met JoAnn and Pokey at Wings and Things on Broad Street.

"Hey, sweetheart, we're over here." Jo Ann said. "Hoss just came by to pick up Missy. She's quite a mess. I overheard him telling her he had to drop her off and then head to the funeral home. I think I heard right. He said to prepare for the body."

"That is strange." Billy Mac frowned. "You'd think the coroner would get dibs first. How are you guys?"

"I never expected this could happen here. Could you tell how that body was suspended up there?"

"No! Our illustrious Police Chief ran me off. He and I don't get on." Billy Mac shrugged.

"Do you think it could be a suicide?" JoAnn asked. "My bets on murder, a bit overboard for suicide, given what you've told me about Jeff, he doesn't seem the type, although this is conjecture only based on what you've told me."

"Murder flashed through my mind as soon as the body dropped." Billy Mac nodded. "My encounter with the body was brief, but it looked as if rigor mortis had set in. I don't believe it's suicide either. My guess is that Jeff was killed yesterday, and the body placed above the stage to be displayed during the party."

"I knew the party was gonna be something, but serving up a murder?" Pokey shuddered. "That's a bit overboard! Anyway, I've got news about Cortez, pretty lame but last night he was here with two other men in a white van. They carried a big trunk into the building through the side door next to the senior's activity building, not the back door with a loading dock. They stayed for one hour and ten minutes and left the way they went in. That was at 2 o'clock this morning."

"You said there were two men with him. What'd they look like?" Billy Mac questioned.

"I had my night binoculars, but they were wearing hoods. About the only thing I got is a description of each, minus the face, of course. One was a big guy, six feet, and well over two hundred pounds. The other guy was about one ninety, approximately five-ten."

"Well, that's not much, but it's a start. Have y'all seen Tank?"

"Not since the party. After I interviewed him about Cortez, I've been meaning to tell you that he invited me to go out with him and Bobbie Jean. We had a great time, really hit it off. They talked about going on a cruise together, them, me and Susan and you and JoAnn. I just wanted to squeeze that bit of fun in before getting back to murder."

"That would be a blast. I knew you and Tank would hit it off, anyway, back to Jeff. This case is not going to be easy. Jeff told me there's a list of people who've wished him dead over the years. Whoever did this wanted there to be no doubt, Jeff was dead. I'm thinking it may be a crime of passion and made it look like a suicide hoping to eliminate any need for a criminal investigation. I just don't understand why it had to be at the party?"

"Do you think it has anything to do with those emails? I know it's unlikely, but those emails did say we'd be sorry, etc. Maybe the killer knew Jeff would be attending and planned to kill him and ruin the event. Of course, that would point to someone living here in town. Of course, it's impossible to tell at this time why he was killed and displayed in this fashion. I certainly don't think we have to worry about any other murders."

"Well, it looks like you both got some good ideas, but it's time for me to bow out of here and leave you two alone. This is some kind of trauma to deal with. I didn't get much sleep last night. I need to go back to the motel to get my beauty sleep. I'll talk to you guys tomorrow."

Billy Mac and JoAnn stopped at his house to get some clothes. As they were walking out the door, his phone rang; it was Tank.

"I was just getting ready to call you. You and Bobbie Jean, okay?"

"'fraid not, I'm on the way to the police station to be interviewed. Booley said there were a lot of people they were going to talk to, and I was a person of interest. Do you think I need a lawyer?"

"Damn, he could have come to your house for that. Do you have an alibi for Friday and Saturday before the party?"

"Yeah, I was working my ass off getting the food ready all-day Friday through Saturday up to the start of the party. I spent Friday night at Bobbie Jean's and left early Saturday morning and went back to work."

"Did Cortez work with you Saturday?"

"Yeah, all day."

"As long as you've got proof of your whereabouts, you've got nothing to worry about. Better I don't show up, seeing as Booley ran me off the crime scene. Call me if he causes you any real trouble. I'm going to get involved in this investigation somehow, despite Booley. Tank, do you happen to know if David Dingler, Jeff's significant other, was there at the party? He was supposed to be Jeff's date?"

"I don't even know what he looks like, but Missy did say something about not seeing Jeff or his date at the beginning of the night."

"Okay, call me as soon as you leave police headquarters."

"Will do."

# # # #

"Tank alright? You look worried."

"He should be fine; Booley's just being Booley."

"You need a massage, and I've got magic hands."

JoAnn started to knead his neck and shoulders.

"Thank you, hon, but we have a lot of work to do."

"I know. Do you want a diet Coke?"

"I do. Why don't you fix yourself a drink?"

"Oh, I am. I think the first thing we need to do is figure out how to circumvent Booley. Right now, I guess we're the self-appointed investigators. He'll block us at every turn unless we have an official status. Should we go to the DA and the sheriff?"

"You've read my mind."

"I've worked with the DA frequently as an expert witness. I'll call him, see when we can go over to see him unless you have a better plan."

"No, call him now, what's his name, Sanders?"

"Yes, Steve Sanders."

JoAnn dialed the number, he answered on the second ring.

"Hey JoAnn, I have been thinking about you, what a horrible tragedy. Are you all right?"

"A little shaken like everyone else. I came up with the idea for the party. Someone has a macabre idea about party crashing. I'll come right to the point for my call. My partner Billy Mac Logan has some information about the case that might be helpful. Booley Lancaster holds a long-time grudge against Billy Mac, ran him off the crime scene, and won't talk with him. We'd like to meet with you as soon as possible to discuss our findings and, hopefully, future involvement."

"Absolutely, seeing as my job is to prosecute the bad guys, I'll take all the good help I can get. When do you want to meet?"

"How about now. This is urgent."

"It's getting late, but I can have the security guard open the courthouse though it may be best to meet somewhere more private."

"How about my house. We're both here now. Do you know where I live?"

"Country Club Estates, right? I've sent deputies there with court paperwork for you before. Just text me the house number; I'm on my way."

"Good memory, see you in a few."

"That's one down. Now, you know Sheriff Brian Langston well, right, Billy?"

"Yes, I've been involved in some mutual cases. I'm gonna ask if he'll deputize us."

"Well, would it help to get a recommendation from the FBI?"

"What? Are you kidding?"

"Nope, I've consulted with them several times. I'm not supposed to tell you, but you are now my soul mate and confidant. I'll make the call."

She went into another room and brought back an encrypted cell phone. "Hey, Marvin, can you name the Three Stooges?"

"Mo, Curly, and Larry."

"Who was the greatest athlete of all?"

"Secretariat, the horse. He had no competition. What's up?"

"I need your help. There's been a murder here in Riverview at an event I helped organize. The murderer made a grand statement having the body fall from above the stage suspended by a cable tied around his leg. This display happened just a few hours ago with all the party-goers watching the stage. Do you remember my mentioning Billy Mac Logan, the private investigator?"

"Yes, you mentioned him a time or two."

"Well, Billy Mac has information the police could use. The victim hired him, but they've, or should I say the Chief of Police, has turned a deaf ear because of a conflict he and Billy Mac had years ago. Would you be willing to call Sheriff Langston and endorse us for deputization? I believe you've worked with the Sheriff on several occasions. Billy Mac is gonna talk with him, but a word from you would go a long way."

"It's a bit of a reach for the FBI to call law enforcement and give recommendations, but for you, JoAnn, I will do it as soon as we hang up."

"Thank you, Marvin. Bye."

"Goodbye."

"Wow!!!! You never cease to amaze me."

# # # #

Within minutes Steve Sanders arrived. As soon as they greeted him, there was a call from Sheriff Langston to JoAnn.

"Hey JoAnn, Brian Langston, I need to talk with either you or Billy Mac."

"Sheriff, Steve Sanders just came in. Let me put you on with Billy Mac."

JoAnn handed Billy Mac the phone as she went to mix Steve a gin and tonic.

"Howdy, Sheriff."

"You got some pretty powerful people endorsing you. But I was going to deputize you anyway. I know you knew the victim, and I never turn away a willing body, especially one with your reputation. I saw how Booley treated you today; guess he's still jealous of you. Just between us, I think he knows you're a better detective."

"I guess we all got our demons. Thanks for your confidence. Can you come over here now? Steve Sanders just got here, and I have some information about the case, might as well say it one time."

"I'm on my way, be there in ten minutes. Just shoot me a text with the address."

Once assembled, the group listened intently as Billy Mac explained his meetings with Jeff Thomas and how he was hired to follow David Dingler. He told them about Jeff's concerns that he may not be safe; and that he was anxious for Billy Mac to get his surveillance started.

Billy Mac told them about following David Dingler on Thursday night and where he ended up. He quickly added he felt it was a random meeting and had nothing to do with the murder. He told the group he had been hired by Zora Benson to shadow Cortez Cortez. And that he had, with her permission, subcontracted the case to the best detective in Vegas, Pokey James. He told them about Cortez's frantic plea to be hired by Tank. How Pokey had seen Cortez and two other men enter the building in the wee hours with a trunk, and finished by saying, "It looks like we have quite a web to weave through."

"Quite a web indeed," said Steve.

"I'm happy to have you guys on my team. Let me swear you in," said the Sheriff.

Chapter 26

Tank's in Jail

JoAnn and Billy Mac were sworn in and handed badges when the phone rang; it was Tank.

"Billy Mac, Booley's putting me in jail!"

"What???"

"Said he wanted to keep me overnight. I told Booley where I was all day. Far as I know, he didn't even check."

"What did he charge you with?"

"He never said anything about charges, Billy Mac."

"I'll be right there. I'm getting you out tonight."

Billy Mac quickly explained what was going on. Steve said he could hold Tank on suspicion but would have to charge him to put him in a jail cell."

"Will you call Booley, Steve and tell him to release Tank. He has no reason to hold him; he has an alibi. I'm gonna go pick him up."

"Okay, go ahead, I'll call."

"JoAnn, I'll be back in a few."

Billy Mac rushed out the door like his feet were on fire!

JoAnn knew Billy Mac was furious; she said a quick prayer that he wouldn't do anything foolish.

Billy Mac pulled up to the City Jail and reached into the Tahoe's glove compartment retrieving the pictures encased in a leather-like folder. He was familiar with the building he was entering. Not only had he worked there, but he also often had business dealings that required him to be in the building. There was a lounge for the officers on the first floor. It had no security cameras. The officers needed a place to relax without feeling they were always watched. The jail itself was located on the fifth floor of the building. A receptionist sat across from the elevator. Someone had to be there round the clock.

"I'm here to see the Police Chief and to pick up Tank Wilson. Tell him Billy Mac Logan's here to see him."

The receptionist hit the intercom button and paged Booley. "Chief Lancaster, you have a visitor in the lobby."

"Who is it?"

"Mr. Logan."

"I'll be right there."

Booley entered the lobby, looking fat, annoyed, and disheveled as usual. He still had on the uniform he wore to the event. There were sweat stains under his armpits, and his too-tight shirt exposed his hairy belly. His stomach hung over his pants that looked like they could fall off at any time. He was a mess.

"You went over my head, didn't you?"

"Look, Booley, I, just like you, want justice. I've got information that could be pertinent to the case. I wanted to show it to you while I wait for Tank."

"Well, show it to me then."

"I will, but first, when is Tank getting out?"

"He's being released in just a few minutes."

"Good, glad you decided to release him. We need to go somewhere really private. Can we use the lounge downstairs? I didn't see anybody in there on the way up here?"

"All right, I need to make a pit stop. I'll meet you there in five minutes."

Billy Mac took the elevator to the first floor. His initial reaction was to threaten Booley after he beat the shit out of him. But now that he had calmed down, he decided the pictures were enough of a threat. And assaulting Booley could backfire on him.

Booley entered the lounge; they were alone.

"What I'm going to show you is just between us, Booley. Jeff Thomas hired me to follow David Dingler. He thought David might be plotting to kill him. Now, of course, Jeff is dead, and David has mysteriously disappeared."

Billy Mac pulled out the first picture of David and Booley's meeting at Wal-Mart. He quickly retrieved it and reached for the second picture showing Booley and David entering Booley's house. Booley had his hand on David's buttocks. Before he showed the last picture, he looked into Booley's eyes. They were filled with horrific fear, and Booley's already pale complexion had turned ghost white. He then showed the last picture of David butt-naked retrieving the paper off of Booley's porch.

"Booley, I'm going to go up and check and see if my buddy is out. I'm sure looking forward to working with you on this case."

Booley just stared with his mouth hanging open, gripping the pictures as Billy Mac left.

Tank did the little 'happy dance' he and Billy Mac had done since high school when something good happened. They would spread their arms wide while running in place and then embrace.

"Need a ride?"

"No, Bobbie Jean is on her way to get me, but I appreciate you comin' down."

"Don't need to thank me, but I gotta get going back to JoAnn's. The Sheriff and DA are there, and JoAnn and I have been deputized. Billy Mac pulled the badge out of his pocket and showed it to Tank.

"Fancy badge, go. Bobbie Jean should be here in a few minutes. We'll talk soon."

# # # #

"You should've seen Booley's face. I put the fear of God in Booley, but I never touched him."

"You showed great restraint, and I'm sure you still made your point quite convincingly," Steve and Brian stayed for about an hour. They are excited to be working with us."

"What about Missy, JoAnn? Have you spoken to her?"

"Yes, Hoss took her down to make an ID of the body before they cremated Jeff."

"What? They have already cremated him?"

"Yes! Brian and Steve were both just as shocked. According to Missy, she took a look at his face, said it was Jeff, and left. She said Booley had plenty of people saying it was Jeff just needed her ID. He told her there wasn't going to be an investigation, and Jeff's Aunt Sophie in Chicago ID him from a picture and said he wanted to be cremated."

"I know I would like to have had another look. There should be an autopsy to confirm suicide if that's what Booley thinks. Of course, an autopsy would confirm our theory of murder. I wonder if Missy will still tell Amanda."

"My guess is she'll probably give it some time."

"We have a lot of investigating to do. Zora needs to be brought up to speed, and then we need to go to Cleveland. Can you go with me?"

"Absolutely, I want to go. We can talk to Zora tomorrow, then leave for Cleveland later in the day. I'll rearrange my schedule."

"Pokey is flying out tomorrow. I thought we'd call to say bye before heading to bed."

"Excellent idea."

# # # #

JoAnn and Billy Mac were in Zora's office at Benson Funeral Home early the next morning to discuss her case.

"Zora, I'm sure you've heard the murder victim was Jeff Thomas. Circumstances have made Cortez a suspect in his murder. We have been deputized as investigators, which I believe alters our contract. I can't continue to investigate Cortez for you. It causes a conflict of interest for me by merging a criminal and civil investigation. Probably the best thing to do is to return your money, at least a portion of it."

"No one had any way of knowing something like this would happen. Hold off on returning any money. In my opinion, you've earned what I gave you. And thanks to my hiring for this job, you now possess an important piece of information about Cortez."

"Okay, we'll let it rest for now, but I think you have some money coming back. Pokey returned to Vegas because now the authorities are keeping an eye on Cortez. There isn't anything more we can do for you."

"I'm still not going to accept a refund."

"Billy Mac and I have to go to Cleveland on business for a couple of days. How about we talk when we return."

"That's fine, but I'm not taking my money back."

They shook hands, and JoAnn and Billy Mac left for Cleveland.

Chapter 27

Aunt Sophie and the Visit to Anna

JoAnn and Billy Mac were on their way to Shaker Heights. They had rented a Nissan Altima at the Cleveland Airport.

"It's hard to get used to this smaller car after driving my Tahoe."

"Somehow, it doesn't fit in Shaker Heights, does it? We should be driving a Volvo."

"Funny, I guess it was one of the most exclusive areas in the States at one time."

The GPS showed 1.2 miles to destination, so they were close. JoAnn looked beautiful. She was wearing a light blue summer dress, dark blue drop earrings, dark blue flats, with a matching purse. Billy Mac wore jeans, a white Polo tee-shirt, and a tan sport coat. He had on his favorite cowboy boots, the medium brown Ostrich ones. They wanted to present as professional but not intimidating.

They parked in the driveway. There was sidewalk leading to the main house and garage. It seemed to wrap around the garage on its way to the former home of Jeff and David. They went up the steps of the large front porch and Billy Mac rang the doorbell. Sophie Myers answered the door wearing designer jeans, a bright green blouse, and heels. At 70 years old, she was still an attractive lady.

"Come on in gorgeous, it's been too long," Sophie kissed him on the lips and hugged him.

Sophie extended her hand to JoAnn. "I have heard about you from Missy. Wow, what a beauty you are."

"Thank you, Ms. Myers, your beauty matches your surroundings."

"Please excuse my brazen embrace of your fellow here. It is not often an old lady gets to squeeze a hunk like that. I remember seeing him a couple of times when William and I visited Riverview. You grew up well."

"I'm having a martini, what is your pleasure, JoAnn?"

"The same, thank you."

"What about you, gorgeous?"

"I'll have a diet coke or water and lemon."

Sophie called out, "Maria?"

Within a couple of minutes a pretty heavy-set woman, probably in her thirties with a warm smile appeared. "I heard the order; I'll get the drinks for you. I'm Maria," and she bowed slightly.

Sophie was an experienced High Society woman thought JoAnn. I'll bet she loved to schmooze and entertain. She likely could keep up with conversation and drinks maintaining an appearance of total control.

When Maria returned, she served the guests first, then Sophie. As Sophie took her drink, she reached into her purse and retrieved a white handkerchief. She took a big sip of the martini, then dabbed her eyes and said tearfully.

"I do declare. I am heartbroken over Jeff. He was a different soul, always an outlaw in his heart, but I loved him. I so enjoyed having Jeff and David live here in the guest house. I just can't believe it. He is, or was, only sixteen years younger than I am, and he is gone. Moreover, according to you Billy, he's been murdered, and in such a gruesome way. And now, David is missing! You have to find out who did this, Billy Mac. JoAnn, I assume you're here to assist him?"

"That is one of the main reasons we are here. Billy Mac has some things to tell you about his conversations with Jeff."

145

"Sophie, Jeff insisted on hiring me to do surveillance and investigate David. He thought David was using him, and that he may have possibly hired somebody to do him harm. He gave me $10,000 and hired me to come here to Cleveland and shadow David. Just so you know, full disclosure, JoAnn is my partner in the agency. We don't feel right keeping money we don't feel we've earned and would like to return his money to you. That is one reason we're here. The other is to get your permission to search their house and ask if you know anything that could help us determine who might want to kill Jeff, besides David."

"No to returning the money. I have an obscene amount of money thanks to the good, smart, hardworking man I married. You keep the money and use it to help with your investigation and if or when you need more, call me, and I'll send it. Money is not an issue and I want this murderer caught. That said, my opinion is that my darling Jeff was feeding you a line of bullshit. He was prone to do that, you know. David could never be a party to violence, even hiring it. I know men, Billy Mac, that boy is nothing but a big pussy. He didn't do it."

"He is missing and nowhere to be found, that is certainly suspicious."

"Oh my! Maybe he's dead too, I just can't believe he'd harm anyone, especially Jeff."

"Oh my, Sophie, it's not our intention to upset you more but is there anyone you know of that could have been threatening Jeff?"

"My darling nephew had many enemies JoAnn. Some of them were here, some in Riverview, and others along the way and who knows where. I couldn't begin to tell you of anyone I would suspect because I'd suspect them all. I loved that boy, but he was a rascal. Jeff was wily as a coyote. You knew him Billy Mac, how charming he could be?

Unfortunately, he never felt guilt or remorse about anything and that leaves a trail of enemies."

"Sophie, would it be okay with you if we searched the guest house? It's a remote possibility, but we might find something connected to the murder."

"Of course, go ahead. I have a wonderful idea, why don't you stay here with me in the house tonight rather than a hotel? I have a wonderful large guest room. Maria keeps it very tidy and guest ready. I enjoy entertaining and often have friends stay the night. I'll have her prepare a lovely dinner. I would enjoy the company."

JoAnn turned to Billy Mac.

"Isn't this a lovely gesture? We haven't checked into a motel yet."

"Then we accept. We'll go search the house and be back with our suitcases as soon as we're done."

JoAnn and Billy Mac made the short trek to the guest house. They conducted a thorough search and JoAnn discovered some letters Jeff had received from someone named Anna. Billy Mac also made a mental note that there were no surveillance cameras.

"I wonder who Anna is? Could she be someone Jeff was seeing?" said JoAnn.

"Maybe, David did suspect he was seeing someone else. Wait a minute, I remember now, when Jeff's mother and father moved back to Cleveland, Jeff's Mom was pregnant."

"That is who Anna must be. Sophie hasn't mentioned her, maybe they don't get along."

"We'll bring it up at dinner. Strange that there isn't a trace of David having ever been in this apartment."

"Except for that picture of David and Jeff. They sure did look alike."

# # # #

"Maria, you are quite a chef."

"Thank you, I love to cook for Ms. Sophie and her guests."

"Billy Mac and I think we're amateur food critics and I believe this is one of the best meals I've ever had and on such short notice. Pork Tenderloin is one of my favorites, and this cornbread is to kill for, oh my, excuse my poor word choice."

"Well, thank you, Ms. Underwood. The cornbread is an old family recipe, and the pork tenderloin was cooked in the Instant Pot, makes for quick dinners. The secret is to sear it on top of the range first, then let it cook for forty-five minutes. Freshly mashed potatoes and green beans go well with about anything and really take no time to prepare."

"It's delicious," added Billy Mac.

Sophie spoke, "Did you find anything in the apartment, JoAnn?"

"Nothing, not even a trace of any David memorabilia. However, we did find some letters from someone named Anna to Jeff."

Sophie turned to Billy Mac.

"Billy Mac, did you know about Anna?"

"No, but after reading the letters, I remembered when your sister moved back here, she was pregnant."

"Yes, Jeff's baby sister was born about thirty-five years ago. That is the one person Jeff seemed to care genuinely care for, if he could care for anyone, such a pity about her condition. Anna is in a mental institution diagnosed with Paranoid Schizophrenia."

"My goodness! What institution is she in?"

"She's here in Cleveland, at the Lanier Clinic. I used to go to see her, but I can't bear it anymore. Jeff went frequently, and she always knew who he was, Jeff said she looked forward to his visits."

"I'm quite familiar with that illness. Do you think it would be possible for us to talk to her? I'll tread with care, but she may be able to shed some light on Jeff."

"Do you really think it would help you find Jeff's murderer? I don't want to upset her if it can be helped."

"Sophie, JoAnn, is an expert in the field of psychology. When you are doing investigative work, you cannot leave a stone unturned, and Anna is a stone."

"Well, alright then, I'll call Dr. Hargrove. The State picks up a lot of her tab, but I send them several thousand dollars a month as well. That should give me some pull. I wouldn't dare stop. The least I can do is make sure she has the best care, and I can afford the best. As I said before, thanks to William, I have plenty of money."

The rest of the evening, Billy Mac and JoAnn tried to lighten the conversation. They asked a lot of questions about Sophie's past life and background. She gladly spoke about herself and revealed to them a fascinating life story.

They also asked her about the history of the house, which Sophie recounted enthusiastically.

# # # #

The Next Morning

Sophie called Lanier Clinic at 8 o'clock. Luckily, Dr. Hargrove was in and agreed to rearrange his schedule to see Billy Mac and JoAnn at 9.

The guests said their goodbyes after an early serving of fruit and yogurt for breakfast. They arrived at the Clinic at 8:45.

JoAnn briefly gave her background and work history, including her stints with the FBI.

Dr. Hargrove was impressed. He instructed the nurses to tell Anna that she has visitors, friends of Jeff's. A nurse came back and reported that Anna is in a receptive mood and delighted.

JoAnn and Billy Mac enter Anna's room. She was sitting in a chair facing them in the corner of the room and had on a Cleveland Brown's sweatshirt. It was oversized and almost covered up the short shorts she was wearing. She had on bright orange walking shoes with ankle-length socks.

Anna is a beautiful girl. Like her brother, she has big round hazel eyes, but the resemblance stops there. Anna's hair is dark, and she wears it short. She is olive-skinned like Jeff but a little darker. She appeared to be like any other young woman her age.

Anna spoke, "I just got through with my exercise."

"You look so fit. I can tell you exercise. Anna, my name is JoAnn, and this is my boyfriend, Billy Mac Logan. He and Jeff were friends and played football together in high school."

"I know you," Anna got up and opened a dresser drawer and pulled out a large scrapbook. She sat down at her desk and opened it.

"Come here." She began to turn to a page of a newspaper clipping. It was a picture of the State Championship Amicalola Blue Devils Football Team.

"That's you. You were number ten, and Jeff," she pointed to Jeff's number, "was eighty."

"Well, I'll be. JoAnn, we were quite a combination, Jeff and me."

"Yes, and y'all were both so cute. Don't you think, Anna?"

Anna nodded.

"Do you get to see Jeff often?" asked JoAnn.

"Oh yes, he comes by every week, and I talk to him almost every day. He called me yesterday and said he was in Riverview."

"Oh, so he is still there?"

"Yes, he is going to take me there one day as soon as it is safe for me to leave here. You don't know, but someone is trying to kill me. Jeff has kept them from hurting me, and that's why I'm here, hiding. But I will be leaving soon."

"Well, when you come to Riverview with Jeff, will you please let us take you to see the falls?"

"Yes, I like you, JoAnn. I bet we could be friends. I just wish those people weren't after me."

"I think it will work out okay, Anna. JoAnn and I have a plane to catch back to Riverview. It has been so nice meeting you and talking to you."

Billy Mac started to get up to leave.

Anna turned to JoAnn, "JoAnn, could I have your phone number? Do you have a business card? You know if it is all right, I will call you sometimes?"

"Please do, Anna. That would be great."

"On the way out, they stopped by to see Dr. Hargrove in his office.

He asked JoAnn for her opinion, even though the meeting was short.

"All of us shrinks know that we can't size somebody without spending a lot of time with them. But what are rules for if not made to be broken? What do you think, JoAnn? I'd value your opinion."

"She does appear to be a textbook case of her diagnosis. She told us that people are out to kill her, but she seems to be missing one element."

"Well, what would that be?"

"Anna does not appear to have that fearful look in her eye as many schizophrenic people do that I have counseled."

"You are astute, Ms. Underwood, my sentiments as well."

"Dr. Hargrove, Anna tells us that she sees and speaks to her brother Jeff often. Do you think that is true?" asked Billy Mac.

"No, we took her phone away a few months ago. He would come by here occasionally to see her, but not as often as she says."

"Well, thank you very much for allowing us to see her doctor," said JoAnn.

On the airplane flight to Birmingham, they both took a restful nap.

Billy Mac dropped JoAnn off at her house. She had counseling sessions tomorrow early, and he had plenty of work to do. He walked her to the door, gave her a big kiss, and exchanged I love you's!

Chapter 28

Role Reversals

Gregory and Amanda were in the second hour of their business meeting in Hoss's office.

Amanda was suggesting some new marketing ideas for the bank. She and Greg had explained to Hoss that they essentially wanted to swap roles and that they were both excited about it. Amanda was to be the businessperson, involved in all aspects of the bank and funeral home, and Greg was the house husband.

Amanda expanded on her ideas for the bank. We need to target older people with money and the medical and professionals in the community. Doctors sure had money.

"Here is what I plan to do. I will be super-charged into going to see people. I'm going to request appointments and build a medical directory to include all the physicians, dentists, and everyone related to the medical community. We will mail them to our existing customers and to anyone who opens an account with us. I also plan to furnish newspapers for everyone in the hospital, as a thank you. I can cut a deal with them down at the Riverview Times. The newspaper business is slowly dying. They will be eager to participate. That is just a start," said Amanda.

"Being super aggressive will benefit us," said Hoss. "I can see that."

"Greg and I will both be happy doing what we want to do. And, the bottom line is, Hoss, we all will make a lot more money. We will have the attorneys change any necessary documents to my name where Greg's is now, or whatever is appropriate. That will be, of course, for the bank and the funeral home."

"Then it's a deal."

Hoss stood up and shook hands with Amanda and Greg.

Chapter 29

Case Discussion

JoAnn called Billy Mac, "I just had an interesting conversation with Amanda."

"Can't wait to hear."

"Do you want me to come over there tonight?"

"There are two excellent reasons for it. One, we need to discuss several things about the case, and two, I have missed you the last couple of days."

JoAnn was at Billy Mac's in thirty minutes after freshening up. She had stationed some clothes, makeup, and a bathroom kit at his home.

When she arrived, she gave him a long and passionate kiss. "A lovely way to start the evening."

They ate turkey and Swiss sandwiches on rye in the dining room. Billy Mac always had smoked meats from Tank's store, "A Cut Above."

"Before we get into discussing the case, I would like your input on how we can handle this. You know how much I appreciate your love for me and making me a partner in your Agency. I always want to be your life partner, and I have a keen desire to work together as a team. However, I still have my practice to consider. I have neglected some people out of necessity as of late. Perhaps neglected is too strong a word. The rescheduling may have inconvenienced them. How can we continue to work together while I take care of my practice?"

"Funny, you should bring that up because I was going to myself. I understand completely. For now, just take care of your practice. I'll move forward, keep you informed, tell you if I need you, seek your advice, and, most of all, love you with all my heart!!!"

Then Billy Mac jumped up and kissed her again.

"Agreed?"

"Agreed."

"Bingo! Now, this is called Billy Mac, thinking out loud. After years of being a detective, I have shared with you not to weigh your instincts against the facts while still finding them. At this point, we have very little in the way of facts. Here are some things that bother me. Number one; we had a very hasty body identification and no autopsy. Two; how did David Dingler just disappear? Three; this is an instinct only, but I have a strong suspicion somebody in the Pitman, and probably more than one person knew that body was going to fall. So, whoever staged that murder was there that night to witness it."

"So, what is the next move? Who do you need to talk to, everyone on the committee?"

"Yes, everyone. I'll continue, but first, what is the news about Amanda?"

"She called me today, very excited. Amanda said she and Greg were 'trading places.' She took over the business interests, and Greg was going to be a house husband and paint. Did you notice the large painting in the den of the beautiful mountains and lakes? Greg did that. And remember, you commented to him about the painting he did from the Auburn Alabama game picture. He is an excellent artist."

"I'm happy for them, and that makes sense. Amanda seems like the left-brainer, and Greg the right-brainer."

"She will be working a lot with Hoss. I don't know what Missy thinks of that."

"I don't either. I doubt she will care.

Okay, smart one, here is what I'm faced with. I was paid by Jeff to watch David, who is now a prime suspect in his murder. I have been paid to watch Cortez Cortez, who may be a murder suspect, as Pokey saw him go into the building in the middle of the night. And, Missy paid me to keep an eye on Hoss, who has a new business partner. And in my mind is also a murder suspect."

"In the meantime, I need to talk to Amanda and Greg, Bobbie Jean and Tank, Emily Scott, and Zora Benson, who happens to be the one paying me to watch Cortez. Of course, I'll need to talk with Hoss and Missy, and Tyrone at Partners."

"That is just for starters. Hon, you have lots of work ahead. Please tell me how I can help."

"You have a good relationship with Zora Benson. You could contact her and tell her that I am still following Cortez and investigating his actions. Also, you could go with me to meet with Brian since we are both deputized. I think it would help if you were with me. You know he was very impressed you were recommended by FBI Agent Marvin Holderfield."

"Okay, which one first?"

"I would like to talk to the Sheriff right away. I need to get into the Pitman."

"Let me call him now."

Chapter 30

Meeting with Sheriff Langston and Tyrone

Billy Mac and JoAnn were in the office of Brian Langston at 9 o'clock sharp Monday morning. Billy Mac explained his concerns about the case and asked for permission to go into the theater. The Sheriff made a phone call to City Hall. A Police Officer would be at the back entrance with a key to the building. Sheriff Langston wanted to go with him. The officer would meet them in about fifteen minutes.

The officer left the key with Billy Mac and the Sheriff to return to City Hall. They entered the building and went up the few steps to the stage. When they got behind the curtain, Billy Mac noticed something he had not seen before. An overhead crane was on a couple of steel rails above them. There was a cable or winch attached to it with a magnet on the end. That cable was the one the body was attached to. However, Greg had said the night of the event that there was a steel beam above. He was probably repeating what Hoss had told him.

"Sheriff, this explains one thing that had been bothering me."

"What's that?"

"Whoever did this wanted a public display of the murder victim. I couldn't figure out how a body could be rigged to fall from a beam at a specified time without somebody being up there to push it off."

"Where did you get the idea the body fell off a steel beam?"

"Greg Sistern mentioned that in the aftermath. But that was a very hectic time. I'm guessing he was probably just guessing or repeating something he heard," said Billy Mac.

"If you are thinking about what I am, those overhead crane magnets can be released remotely."

158

"Exactly! With a key fob, as long as it is not too far from the magnet."

"I agree, Billy Mac. I'm almost one hundred percent sure we are right. But just in case I know an expert, we can check with Talmadge Mullins of Mullins Crane."

"Yes, I know, Talmadge. He would be knowledgeable about that. This corroborates what my instincts were saying. Somebody in the building that night committed or knew about the murder. This is definitely not a suicide."

"Do you think a member of the POETS may have been involved?"

"The short answer is yes, but that is pure instinct with no facts and nothing to back that up. But it would make sense as committee members had access to the Pitman."

"Have you talked to Booley?"

"Yes, I think he will be more cooperative going forth."

Brian grinned, "I won't ask."

Billy Mac took the key back to City Hall, and then he crossed the river to Partners.

"Tyrone, Billy Mac Logan here," as he extended his hand.

"I was expecting somebody from the City Police. Then again, maybe I wasn't. We have met before, haven't we, Billy Mac?"

"Yes, several years ago, when you first bought the bar. My work brought me here. Now it looks like it has come full circle!"

"Can I get you something to drink? Seems to me it was diet coke, wasn't it?"

"I believe I'll splurge and have one."

"Tina, watch the bar for me, please. Let's go back to my office, Billy Mac."

Tyrone handed Billy Mac the coke while walking to the office.

Tyrone's office was tastefully decorated. There was a big leather sofa, a leather recliner, and a television. A large glass desk had a swivel chair behind it and a comfortable chair in front. A small kitchenette had a coffee maker, and there was a full bath with a shower.

"Nice office, Tyrone."

"I work a lot. Sometimes I sleep here rather than locking up and going home; it seems like such a waste of time."

"I'm sure you have heard the news. A murder suspect by the name of David Dingler is missing. We think he may have been in here last Thursday night. Was he, and did you meet him?"

"Yes, and yes. I had a conversation with him, a pretty boy from Cleveland. He conversed with several of our regulars for a while and left around 10:30."

"Do you know where he went? Did he say anything that may have indicated what his plans were for the night?"

"Are you working with the Sheriff's office? I heard you were, just wanna be sure I won't find myself having trouble with the police."

"Yes."

Billy Mac pulled out his badge and credentials showing them to Tyrone.

"He came in here early Thursday evening around 6. He told me who he was, who he had come to Riverview with, and for what reason. He then went on to tell me that he was soon breaking up with his partner Jeff and that he was interested in finding another partner. He told me he had just been approached by a man in the parking lot and described him. Asked me if I knew who it may have been. I told him that it sounded like the MO of someone that trolled this area. We run a respectable bar here, Billy Mac."

"You certainly do from what I have heard people say. You have been very forthright with 'em. Was the man in question by any chance Booley Lancaster?"

"Yes. We don't like him hanging around here, he is not well-liked by the clientele, but he is the police chief."

"What is your opinion of your brief encounter with David Dingler? Do you think he could be capable of murder?"

"I don't believe that boy could kill anybody. You never know, but I don't know why he would come in here and broadcast to a stranger that he was breaking up with someone he was planning to murder before he murdered him. Doesn't make sense, does it? Just my opinion, and I'm pretty good with people."

"I can see you are. Have you ever had any interest in detective work?"

"Matter of fact I have: my brother is a PI in Atlanta."

"I'll keep that in mind. Thanks for the diet coke and the information."

"I'll always shoot straight with you, Billy Mac. I bet you knew everything I told you before you came in here, didn't you?"

Billy Mac smiled and shook his hand goodbye.

Chapter 31

Missy

Billy Mac punched in Missy's number.

"All things considered, how are you holding up?"

"I just take extra medication. You know most of us women my age do. When in doubt, double up! Just kidding, I don't have a drug problem."

"I've heard exercise is cheaper and may work better."

"I need a partner; you available?"

"No, I already have a partner I exercise with."

"Well, I guess that could be called a resounding no! She's a lucky woman."

"Missy, JoAnn, and I have been deputized by the Sheriff to assist in solving Jeff's murder. Because of the nature of the crime and the new role I am playing, I can no longer help you with Hoss. It's not that I don't want to help, but I feel it would be a conflict of interest. I need to give you back what I didn't pay Pokey since I'm off the case. Where can I meet you to give you the money, and in what form do you want it?"

"You found out what I wanted to know. There is no need to return any money. I'm more than satisfied with what you found. I'm just bummed, Billy Mac. I'm sorry."

"Why don't you talk to JoAnn if you feel the need?"

"I may do that."

"Missy, do you feel like answering some questions about Hoss and his relationship with Jeff? And any other questions I may have?"

"Go ahead, let's do it now. I'll tell you what I know, which isn't much."

"Missy, anything we discuss now must be in the strictest of confidence, okay

"You have my word. I'll button my lips."

"Good, did you have any contact or know anything about David Dingler, who was living with Jeff?"

"No, Jeff told me about him when he said he was coming. I didn't ask any questions. That's all I know."

"What was the relationship Hoss had with Jeff? Hoss knows about Amanda, right

"Hoss never seemed to mind about Jeff. Of course, you know that Amanda and Greg own a considerable share of Moyer Cutler Funeral Home. It's like I have said before, Hoss doesn't seem to care about anyone or anything except making money. His main purpose in having it seems to be so he can have sex orgies and spend it on other women, and of course me.

To answer your question about his relationship with Jeff, I'm not sure. I don't think it was adversarial. I think he and Jeff have done some business, but I'm not sure what."

"Are you speaking of the funeral business, and why do you think that?"

"Jeff worked for some company that sold caskets, or so I was told when I overheard Hoss talking to him. I inquired about it, and I was abruptly told this by Hoss, who was implying, don't ask any more questions, Missy."

"Just to confirm what I think you said, Hoss was speaking with Jeff on the phone. Hoss confirmed it was Jeff Thomas he was speaking with and that maybe Jeff was a casket salesman. Did I get that right?"

"Yes, you got it right, Billy Mac."

"Did Hoss ever talk to you about the funeral home or anybody that worked there?"

"Never! Like I said before, he didn't even like for me to ask about it. If I ever do, he is flippant and dismissive in his response, just like he was when I asked about Jeff."

"So, he never mentioned Cortez Cortez then?"

"Once. One day we were having a drink, and he raised his glass in a toast and said, 'to my little Mexican, Cortez Cortez, well done.' Hoss had consumed about six scotches when he did that. Then he said, 'to the festival' and I said what festival. Then he said, 'any festival.' And that's about as close to an attempt at humor I have ever heard from Hoss."

Billy Mac ended his conversation with Missy. He hoped he had not been too brusque with her. He felt sorry for her, living with a man she can hardly stand, having a daughter as a friend but needing to keep it a secret. However, her flirting bothered him. It made him feel like he was somehow cheating on his relationship with JoAnn. It also reminded him of a past he did not want to revisit.

He did learn something from Missy that could be important to the case. All he could do now is file it away for possible future reference. Jeff had told him he was a day trader. Missy was told he was a casket salesman, just another inconsistency. Billy Mac purposely did not ask about Amanda and Greg switching roles. Maybe he should have, he thought. But surely Amanda will tell her if she hadn't already.

Chapter 32

JoAnn and Zora

JoAnn had Zora on the phone.

"Zora, when we invited you to the party, it was supposed to be just that, a party. I'm so sorry for what you had to witness, a horror show. I feel terrible for everybody concerned; this whole party thing was my idea."

"Now, you are the psychologist. You know what you would tell a patient JoAnn. It's not your fault!! Of course, I must admit, I see a lot of dead people, but they are not presented like that."

"It was lurid! It was so glaringly vivid, and graphic. Zora, Billy Mac, and I have been deputized by the Sheriff to aid with the investigation. He has not interviewed Cortez yet. So, we only know what we reported to you earlier about him being sighted entering the building in the middle of the night. As you were told, he was carrying, or helping carry, what appeared to be a large trunk. Since he is now a murder suspect, I trust you will keep this information in confidence.

Zora, this changes everything. You gave Billy Mac quite an advance. I know he would like to refund you part of that. We just don't know where we are professionally and ethically at this time."

"I don't need the money back. Just keep doing what y'all do. I trust it will be the right thing, and you may still be able to answer my query as well."

Chapter 33

Dinner with Tank and Bobbie Jean

"I miss you!" said JoAnn. "I guess we are both workaholics."

"Yeah, as we use to say at Amicalola High, we are as wide open as a case knife. Why don't you spend the night at my place tonight? Let's take Tank and Bobbie Jean to dinner?"

"Great idea. Give them a call, and I'll get ready!"

The four of them were seated at Porky's, Billy Mac's favorite BBQ restaurant.

"Billy Mac, you should have brought Pokey here to eat when he was in town. You could have taken a picture of him standing outside the restaurant. That way, the caption would be Pokey at Porky's". He mouthed yuk, yuk, yuk.

"What's that TV show? The World's Worst Comedians?"

"That boy is clever, Bobbie Jean. Just like old Billy Mac. They could be a tag team wrestling on the senior tour, funny and funnier," exclaimed JoAnn.

They all chuckled.

"I guess we could all use a laugh," said Billy Mac. "Tank, have you heard from Cortez?"

"No, but I have something that I just found out that I was going to tell you tonight."

"Cortez helped me prepare for that event. I just about bit off more than I could chew preparing for five hundred folks. I'm not complaining; Greg paid us well. That Friday, we worked all day solidly; and Cortez and one of his buddies and I delivered some food there in the wee hours Saturday morning. That helped take a load off all that food we had to deliver right before the party started.

While we were working together, I had to tell Cortez I could not use him full-time. He seemed really disappointed, even frightened. About two hours ago, I called his house. We have had several catering orders, and I need him next week, but he is nowhere to be found."

"You mean his family doesn't know where he is?" asked JoAnn.

"He's disappeared. Nobody knows his whereabouts."

"Tank, you said that food was delivered early Saturday morning. Where did you enter the building?" asked Billy Mac.

"The side door. We were supposed to go in the back, but we had been given the wrong key. We had to go up those steps next to the Senior Activity building with a trunk. It wasn't easy."

"Did you notice anything unusual about the stage area where the body fell from Saturday night?"

"No, we were there about twenty minutes, tops. We unloaded the trunk into a freezer that was already there. It was the frozen veggie items and some desserts."

"Bobbie Jean, I don't guess you noticed anything or anyone unusual regarding the parking and outside?"

"Nothing unusual, the parking before the party was extremely well executed. One thing surprised me a little, but then I'm no expert on crime. That's your department, Billy Mac.

What I'm referring to is how quickly they got Jeff's body out of there. We were trying to do a little crowd control and maintain order. It caused a little bit of turmoil when they brought the body out of the theater's back door so soon. They didn't even let the crowd disperse or the parking lot empty."

"That was quite unusual to spend that little time on a crime scene. You're right, Bobbie Jean."

"JoAnn and I are going to try to earn the badges we received from Sheriff Langston."

"Billy Mac has got a great detective mind. I hope I can be some help. Do you have any idea where Cortez could have gone, Tank?"

"No, but JoAnn, don't you speak Spanish?"

"Yes, Tank, I do."

"I would start with a couple of buddies that are tight with him. I can get you their names. One of them helped with the food."

After dinner, JoAnn and Billy Mac spent a sensual and exhausting hour catching up on their sexual activity. Afterward, they cuddled. Spending time together like this helped them have better focus.

"Now we know as suspected that was Tank with Cortez delivering food, not a body to the building. I think I can help with Cortez Billy Mac."

"Yes, I know. Let's go together as soon as you can and pursue finding Cortez's friends. I hope no harm has come to him."

"What should I tell Zora about this, or should I, as you say, Billy Mac, keep it down-home?"

"Keep it down-home. Why is Cortez afraid of his job at the funeral home; and why are they suspicious of Cortez. Something's not right, and money doesn't seem to be an issue with anyone who has hired me lately. It just keeps getting thrown around!"

"Are you suspicious of Zora and Missy?"

"More so of Zora. I was also suspicious of Jeff. I think Missy is legit, but I'm not ruling anything out. I'm not accusing anyone either, just brainstorming."

Chapter 34

Meeting with Eduardo and the Cortez Family

JoAnn and Billy Mac met with Cortez's best friend Eduardo, who spoke broken English. Cortez and Eduardo have been friends since childhood in Mexico and entered the country together. Tank arranged the meeting.

JoAnn spoke, "Estamos aqui porque queremos ayudar a tu amigo?" We are here because we want to help your friend."

"Si, te creo." (Yes, I believe you.)

"Cortez queria salir defuneral, porque," (Why did Cortez want to leave the funeral home?)

"Cortez mutilar o profaner el cuerpo. Oreia que dios le castigaria." (They made him mutilate or desecrate the bodies, and he thought God would punish him.)

"Que le saber hacienda al Cuerpo?" asked JoAnn. (What was he doing to the bodies?)

"Fara cortado, fara cortado," Eduardo made an outline around his face. (Cut off the face, cut off face).

Further questioning of Eduardo revealed that he was fearful for Cortez. He said Cortez would never leave without telling him and his family where he was going. Billy Mac requested that JoAnn tell Eduardo not to mention this conversation or what he knew to anyone else, no one. She did that, and Eduardo said he would tell no one, not even his wife. JoAnn told him that would be the safest.

Billy Mac knew that was all Eduardo knew; they thanked him and headed home.

"In my practice, in all these years, I thought I had heard almost everything. But Billy Mac, I must admit, I do believe I'm in shock. Do you really think Cortez was cutting faces of off corpses, and if so, why?"

"I'm thinking about having a drink right now. That's how shocked I am. In answer to your question, I have no idea!"

"We need to go home, chill, and pray, and see what happens next. In my experience, prayer will lead us to where we need to go with this investigation."

JoAnn and Billy Mac did just that; they chilled by meditating and praying together. The next morning, they went for an early run, a two-mile jog. Being the lady she was, she thought about allowing Billy Mac the honor of finishing first. But, being the competitor she was, she wanted to make this a race.

JoAnn ran regularly and competed in lots of 5k's. She was an 880, mile runner and high jumper on the track team in high school. Plus, she was twelve years younger than Billy Mac.

Though fit in his early years, Billy Mac now ran infrequently, so his pace was a jog. Even though he worked out with weights and played racquetball, he wasn't used to two-mile runs.

JoAnn set a leisurely pace. She could run the distance in under fourteen minutes, but her pace was for about twenty. Billy Mac started picking up the pace after one mile. JoAnn matched him shoulder to shoulder and began to chuckle silently to herself. She would toy with him until the last one-eighth of a mile. She figured Billy Mac had sealed his fate. His taking over as pacesetter had made this a competition.

Billy Mac was beginning to suffer, but he was tough. The pace was torrid for him. He continued to press on. His breathing was rapid, and he was beginning to really tire. At that moment, with about a fourth of a mile remaining, JoAnn hit another gear, the one meant for champions. She literally dusted Billy Mac, leaving him lagging far behind.

Finishing the run, they were both soaked with sweat. She figured she would make up her rough treatment of him in the shower, and that she did.

After the shower, she treated Billy Mac to a three-egg, cheese, mushroom, onion, tomato, and olive Mediterranean Omelet. Rye bread slightly toasted, and steaming coffee completed the breakfast. There were a couple of giant strawberries to clean the palate afterward.

The run helped relax them along with the activities afterward.

They were sitting on JoAnn's back porch, both in shorts and tee-shirts, enjoying the breeze and ceiling fan.

"I have every confidence, Billy that you will figure this out. You know I will help any way I can."

"We will figure it out together. I knew from the beginning that this whole landscape has puzzle pieces that just don't fit. The haste to cremate Jeff makes no sense. All these people are intertwined in business. That is a little unusual, mixing a bank with a funeral home. And Jeff running a line of bull shit on me, I don't believe David had plans to kill him. Jeff lied about having surveillance cameras placed in the house.

Oh, and JoAnn, you know how people are about money. Even people with a lot of money are not real loose with it. Here I've been given $30,000 total, for starters, they said. Just keep the money, Billy Mac, they have all said. It makes no sense; they've all got to be in cahoots. Think about it. Each one has a seemingly separate but suspiciously similar case and lots of money to hire us. I think they're trying to throw us off the trail. You never got to meet Jeff, JoAnn, but what is your take on all these other folks we have spoken with.

"I do not trust Missy. I'm trying to convince myself that I'm not just jealous of her because of your past relationship, but I don't think that is it, just instinct. An easier way to say it is that the only people to exclude as a suspect besides us on the committee would be Tank and Bobbie Jean.

"That is about the way I'm thinking. Something is going down at Moyer Cutler that is not kosher, and I don't know yet what the bank has to do with it. I don't think Missy knows anything, and that is not coming from my past. I have not spoken to Emily Watts, and I should. Nor have we pursued Greg and Amanda. It may be better if we ask the Sheriff to speak with Hoss and Missy."

"That's a good idea, Billy. After all, he is the Sheriff. He has to be included although, I'm sure you are a better detective. Not that I'm biased or anything! Plus, you were hired by Missy to get dirt on Hoss, and that could be seen as a huge conflict of interest if they are involved."

"How is your work going in your practice? You are still pretty slammed, aren't you?"

"Thankfully, yes. But you know I'll do anything you ask me to."

"Yes, I know. Just concentrate on your practice right now. I will need you to go with me and speak to Cortez's family. Or maybe not, I've heard his children speak English very well. He has a boy and a girl, and they are both in high school. Let me just try it alone. I will call you if things are not going well, and you can get on the phone with them."

Billy Mac left JoAnn's and called Tank. He wanted directions to Cortez's home and told Tank he wanted to arrive there, unannounced. Cortez lived in the Mill Village, a development of houses built for the workers at the old Cotton Mill way back in the 40s and 50s. They were good and sturdy homes but far from fancy. Most had been well cared for by the residents.

Cortez's house was white with green awnings and windowsills. The yard was immaculately clean and beautifully landscaped. Billy Mac guessed the inside of the home would be as well kept. He parked in the driveway and walked up three steps to the porch and front door.

Shortly after ringing the doorbell, a young girl of about sixteen came to the door. Right behind her was a boy, probably her brother, who looked to be a couple of years younger. He greeted them in English and showed them his badge.

The girl introduced herself as Luciana and her brother as Juan Carlos.

"Nice to meet you. I'm Billy Mac Logan. Is your mother home?"

"No, she has gone to meet with Mr. Hendricks. He is supposed to help us find our father," said Luciana. "I'm not comfortable asking you in without Mama here, but I will talk to you on the porch."

"Well, that is what I want to do, find your dad. I am a good friend of Tank Wilson. I do not know your father well, but I know he is a good man."

"Thank you. We are worried about him."

Juan Carlos interrupted the conversation.

"Do you think someone may have abducted him? I don't think he would just run away without telling us."

"It is possible, of course. It's also possible that he was frightened by something or someone. Do you think he could have just gone away for a few days?"

Joan Carlos shook his head no. Luciana answered.

"Not my father. He would never leave without telling us."

Billy Mac just received a text from JoAnn that made a loud, whooshing sound. It said, call ASAP, 911.

"Excuse me for just a moment, please, while I make a call."

"Okay."

He stepped down to the lawn and called JoAnn.

"I'm with Cortez Cortez's kids. Are you okay?"

"Billy, I'm all right, a little shocked! I just got a phone call from Anna Thomas in Cleveland. Remember, she asked for my card before we left her. I asked her, Oh, I didn't know you had a phone, my dear. She replied Dr. Hargrove doesn't know either. I hide it behind the air vents in that tubing. You won't tell him, will you?"

"I promised I would not tell. Billy Mac, I recorded the call. She said she heard from her brother Jeff. I recorded her conversation. Would you like to hear it now or later?"

"I'll finish up here and be right over."

Billy Mac, a little unnerved, continued his conversation with the kids.

"Can either of you tell me anything that might help me find your father?"

"Our Father did not like working at the funeral home anymore. I'm sure of that," said Luciana.

"What changed? He worked there for years. Juan, do you know?"

"No, he would not tell us anything. I don't think he told Mother anything either. But he acted worried."

"Why did your mother go see Mr. Hendricks?"

"He called and asked her to come down to the funeral home," said Luciana.

"I promise I will work hard to find him. Could you please call me after you have talked to your mother?"

"Yes, sir, we will," said Luciana.

"Do you mind if I say a little prayer that we find your father?"

"Not at all, please do," Luciana answered for both of them.

Billy Mac reached out and took each of the kid's hands as they formed a circle, "Dear God, we ask that you keep Cortez safe, and we seek your guidance in finding him. Please help Luciana and Juan Carlos and Mrs. Cortez. Keep their faith and trust in you while we search for him, and may they remain in peace. Amen."

Chapter 35

The Recording of Anna

"Okay, here goes," JoAnn said as Billy Mac pushed the play button. "The conversation picks up after she told me about hiding the phone."

"JoAnn, I had a wonderful call from Jeff today. I love hearing from him so much. I told him about you and Billy Mac coming by to see me and how nice y'all were. He said that was great. He said he knew Billy Mac in high school and that he caught a lot of passes from Billy Mac. Jeff said they were undefeated and won the State Championship."

"How exciting! Are you sure it was Jeff?"

"Positive, I know his voice well. And besides, he knew the secret word, and we always have to ask the secret word before we talk. I'll tell you what it is, JoAnn, but I don't want you to tell anyone else."

"Not even Billy Mac?"

"Not even Billy Mac."

"Okay, it's just between us girls."

"It's 'virgin,' you know, because I'm a virgin."

"Well, that's a good thing."

"He asked me about you, and he said you're Billy Mac's girlfriend."

"Yes, I am. Did Jeff say anything else about us? Should we try and see him?"

"No, I don't have his number. He said because of the people that are trying to kidnap me that he could only call me. That way, a call could not be traced."

"I think I understand. Did Jeff say when he would call again?"

"He never tells me that. JoAnn, I have to exercise now. Before they come into my room, I have to hide my phone. Goodbye."

"Goodbye, please call again."

JoAnn turned off the recording and looked at Billy Mac.

"This is either getting more complicated, or we are beginning to put the pieces of the puzzle together. I wish I knew which."

"You are underestimating yourself, Billy. We have come a long way in gathering information."

Chapter 36

Cortez's Return

Billy Mac's phone rang. "Hello, this is Billy Mac."

"Hi, this is Luciana, Mr. Logan. I wanted to let you know that all is well; my father is home. Mother spoke with Mr. Hendricks, and they found him. They don't want to say anymore. Whatever misunderstanding he and Mr. Hendricks had is settled. He is going to go back to work at the funeral home, and he got a raise."

"What good news, Luciana. I'm grateful he is okay. Thank you for calling to let me know. Goodbye."

"This does not compute."

"No, absolutely not. I'm happy he is alive. I'm afraid he is being blackmailed, or worse, physically threatened. Why don't we get some food to take to Cortez and flowers for his wife and pay them a surprise visit? To celebrate his being safe."

"Come on, let's go by Tank's for the food, and we will pick up some flowers at Publix."

Forty-five minutes later, Billy Mac and JoAnn were at the little home in Mill Village.

This time Mrs. Cortez answered the doorbell. She looked a little startled, and they detected a fearful look in her eye.

JoAnn spoke, "We did not come to stay, Mrs. Cortez, but we are so excited that Cortez is back. We brought you some lovely flowers, and we have some food for your family, so you don't have to cook tonight. Could we just give Cortez a big hug? Nos gustaria darle infuerte abraza a Cortez!"

Alejandra Cortez was skittish, but she was mannerly. She invited them in and called Cortez.

"There he is," cried Billy Mac as Cortez entered the room. He was freshly shaven and looked as if he had just come out of the shower. Juan Carlos and Luciana were right behind him.

"We want to hug you, you first, JoAnn."

JoAnn gave him a big hug, "You're safe; we're so glad you're safe, and so is Tank."

Billy Mac was next. He hugged him, saying, "Glad you are back, old friend."

"Gracias, Billy, I be fine."

JoAnn and Billy Mac conversed for a few minutes with the Cortez family before leaving.

"What were your impressions, JoAnn?"

"I think the funeral homeowners are holding something over their heads. I did not see any kind of epiphany having occurred. They aren't at peace, but they've accepted their status, whatever that might be. All their body language pointed to that."

"I want to put a tracking device on Hoss's car. We need to check if the Sheriff has spoken with Hoss and Missy. I was hoping he would've called us by now. By the way, I don't want to tell him about the tracking device, not now."

"Why don't we call the Sheriff when we get home, Billy?"

Chapter 37

Reporting to the Sheriff

"Hey, Sheriff, JoAnn Underwood."

"I would recognize those lovely tones anywhere. How are you and Billy Mac?"

"We are a little frazzled but are beginning to put some things together. Here's some news! Cortez is back home. Billy and I visited his home and saw him. Billy Mac had been by earlier to interview his family. Then they called him and said Cortez had returned. Cortez's wife, Alejandra, had been to talk with Hoss Hendricks, who must have played a part in this somehow. Cortez is back home from wherever he has been, but it is obvious they are hiding something."

"That is big news. I have spoken with Hoss and Missy. I had it on my planner to call you guys tomorrow. Hoss said that they felt like they had undisputable identification from several people that it was Jeff's body, and Booley agreed. His wishes to be cremated were in writing; therefore, there was no reason to wait. The coroner ruled his death as death by suffocation. His air supply had been cut off, probably due to being hung."

With regard to Cortez, Hoss said he thought he was probably involved somehow with drugs. His past as a recovering drug addict was all Hoss needed to make the statement. He felt like Cortez slipped every once in a while, and that he would return. Missy said she knew nothing about anything. She did mention she had called you to say that Jeff never contacted her after he arrived in Riverview. I wish I had something, but I left there with what the bird left on the pump handle."

"The effort wasn't wasted at all, Sheriff. Now we have their statements on record, and we certainly needed that. It is also fairly apparent to me that Cortez is at least not doing drugs. Sheriff, I suspect something illegal is going on at Moyer Cutler, but my gut instinct won't get us a search warrant, will it?"

"Nope, that would be a question for DA Steve, but I don't think so."

"Is there anything we can do directly for you, Sheriff Langston?" asked JoAnn.

"Just keep on keeping on. We will all figure this out at some point. Somebody involved is bound to make a mistake."

Billy Mac and JoAnn hung up the phone. They decided to spend the night in their own homes. They needed a good night's rest and to catch up on any work they had put aside.

Chapter 38

Abduction Foiled

JoAnn awakened from a restful night's sleep. She took a shower, dried her hair, put on a little makeup, and made a phone call. Vanessa answered. That was her self-imposed job. John had a cell of his own, but he rarely turned it on except to check his messages daily.

"Hey Mom, I want to take you guys out to breakfast this morning at that new Original Pancake House."

"How long do we have to get ready?"

"Can you be there at 8:30?"

"Yes, dear, your dad will be excited. See you shortly."

Good, that will give me time to run to Winn Dixie and get some items first, thought JoAnn.

Her house's wooded area protected her privacy and was hardly visible from the road. She put on some freshly ironed shorts and a blouse and grabbed her purse.

As she walked outside, her thoughts turned to Billy Mac. She was thinking and thanking God silently for that man, and was not paying close attention to her surroundings. She hit the garage door button and hit the key fob to unlock the Volvo. As she opened the car door, suddenly, her purse was pulled from her arm.

From behind, someone quickly reached up under her arms and strong hands clasped behind her neck, holding her in a full nelson. Instinctively she jumped off the ground, throwing her arms straight up in the air, breaking the hold her assailant had on her. As she came down, she fast and furiously jabbed her left elbow backward. She hit paydirt as she felt her elbow go into his genitals. He cried out a painful groan.

Taking advantage of the moment, she used her right elbow, smashed it into the big fellow's nose, feeling and hearing cartilage breaking, the man went down. Behind him, another man charged toward her wielding a knife. Thanks to her martial arts training, she just managed to avoid being badly cut.

This attack was all taking place in the cramped quarters between the garage and the wall, giving her limited mobility. The man still had the knife. She had stepped over the man writhing on the ground, thanks to her quick reflexes. Her instinct told her she would have to charge Mr. Knife to inflict some damage. Hopefully, she could dislodge the knife from his hand. JoAnn knew that her best course of action was to run. She had nowhere to go but through him. She picked up her purse, swung, and walloped him on the hand. She broke the skin, but he held the knife steadfastly. She jumped, turning sideways, and kicked him in the chest. The man stumbled backward, losing his balance. She quickly charged and administered another kick aimed at his chin; she connected.

Unfortunately, as the man fell, he held on to the knife, and it came up, stabbing her in the buttocks. She felt the wetness and knew she was bleeding, but no pain, at least not yet, her adrenaline was running too high. She bolted over the downed man and ran, purse in hand, down the steep wooded hill behind her house to the street, and it was downhill all the way.

On the way down the hill, she was tearing through bushes and briars, fast. Once she reached the street, she pulled out her phone and called 911 for an ambulance, saying she had been stabbed. The ambulance was there before she was able to call Billy Mac, which she did from the gurney.

The EMTs placed her face down on the gurney, hoisted it into the ambulance, and took off siren blaring and lights flashing. The EMTs began treating the wound on the way to the hospital.

# # # #

Riverview Regional Hospital

Billy Mac and the Underwood's arrived at the Emergency room at the same time. The nurse let them know that JoAnn was being x-rayed and instructed them to sit in the ER waiting room. The ER nurse was a former student and admirer of Vanessa and gave more information than she normally would to another family. She told them that the prognosis looked promising, and the doctor would be out soon to speak with them.

The doctor appeared only a few minutes after and informed the group there did not appear to be anything but a deep flesh wound. She had several scratches and lacerations from running down the hill through the woods. All would heal, and there should be no lasting effects physically, except maybe a scar, from the attack. Since they had not heard JoAnn's account of the incident, they didn't know how grave it could have been.

Billy Mac called the Sheriff immediately to report the incident. Not long after, Langston texted back, saying the assailants were in custody. He asked if Billy Mac would come to interview them with him. Billy Mac replied that he would after he had seen JoAnn.

By this time, JoAnn was assigned a room and was settled in. Vanessa and John, per Billy Mac's insistence, went in to see her first. He thought that to be the right thing to do, parents should always take precedence, and Vanessa was quite worried. In about fifteen minutes, John came out and got Billy Mac.

As Billy Mac walked in, JoAnn smiled and said, "My hero."

"No, you are my hero," he said as he reached over to kiss her.

"Oh, no, don't tell me we are going to break out in song?"

As soon as she stopped laughing, she began to give the details of the attack. She began by saying she felt grateful to be alive and to have avoided serious injury. She felt the original intention of the perpetrators was to abduct her, though she had no thoughts as to why, or what they would gain. She told them how the first assailant had put her in a full nelson and how she reacted. Then things went awry when she got away from the first guy. She went on to recount how she handled the second assailant, and that she named him knife guy. That got a small chuckle from the room. She ended her account with the observation that they obviously had no idea who they were messing with.

After spending some time with JoAnn and the Underwoods, Billy Mac said his goodbyes. He explained he was asked to be in the interrogation room when they were being interviewed. The doctor insisted on keeping JoAnn overnight for observation in case of any injury-related issues. He just wanted to verify that she was all right. She insisted that Billy Mac leave and work the case, but she expected him to pick her tomorrow up upon her release.

As Billy Mac drove to the County Jail, he burst into tears, sobbing heavily. This was his fault. He should never have brought her into this dangerous territory.

The cry was good for him. It released the stress he was feeling. By the time he had pulled into the jail headquarters, he had regained his composure, and a calm feeling descended on him.

Chapter 39

Interrogating Suspects

Billy Mac quickly told the Sheriff and DA Sanders JoAnn's recount of the incident. Sheriff Langston gave him leave to interrogate the suspects alone while he observed through the two-way window. Billy Mac inquired about the legality of any information he obtained. The Sherriff let him know that as he deputized him, everything would be admissible in court.

Billy Mac had no problem with that and entered the interrogation room. First up was the big fellow who had a broken nose and some real sore genitals. He was holding an ice pack between his legs.

Billy Mac pulled up a chair and looked across the table at the man of about three hundred pounds, probably six feet two or three inches. He had an unusually large head and a round puffy face, which was black and blue around the eyes from the broken nose. He looked downright miserable.

"I'm Billy Mac Logan, Deputy Sherriff, and Private Investigator. What's your name?"

"Carl Chamblers."

"Where do you live?"

"Tennessee."

Billy Mac gave Carl a long stare. "Carl, don't you give me any bullshit answers! I'm in a position to help you help yourself. Do you know the penalty for attempted murder in Alabama?"

"I didn't try to kill nobody, I swear!"

"Carl, here's the deal. Listen to me very carefully. There is a big difference between an attempt to murder and murder. Then you got aggravated assault. That's not as bad, but God helps you if that girl in the hospital dies. The best thing I could do for you then, Carl, is to buy you a couple of cases of Vaseline to take to jail with you. Cause you'd be there a long time unless they executed you. You know what I mean, Carl?"

"I don't know about assault, that chick did a number on me. All I did was grab her from behind. I seen Wilbur with a knife, even though I was on the ground, I was tryin' to keep an eye on the girl. It wasn't supposed to be like that. We was supposed to bring her up to the RV Park. We was gonna gag her and all, but when she started pummeling me, Wilbur went crazy. I didn't have no weapon. I done it for the money, $500 bucks. I didn't want to hurt nobody!"

"Who paid you?"

"I swear, I don't know! Wilbur done the negotiations. He said he didn't know who the man was. He had some kind of machine making his voice sound funny on the phone, kind of like Darth Vader. Wilbur never met him. It was all by phone. The man found Wilbur and called him."

"I'm leaving this room now, Carl. I'm going to talk to your white trash friend Wilbur, see what that piece of shit has to say. He better have a similar story. In the meantime, I want you to write all this down for the Sherriff word for word and answer any questions he may ask you. Be specific, Carl. Not like when you said, I live in Tennessee. You tell them exactly where you live and every little detail they ask. I think that maybe you're telling me the truth. If so, I can help you, maybe get a reduced sentence, or even keep you out of jail. Do you understand me, Carl? Whoever sings first will be the winner."

"Yes, I do, I do!"

Billy Mac stepped out of the room. "Great work, too bad you're not a permanent member of the force," said Brian. He and Steve Sanders had been listening to the interrogation.

"Agreed, you're skilled," said Steve.

"One down and one to go. I'm ready for Wilbur. Still want me to have a go at him alone?"

Sherriff Langston and Steve both nodded in agreement.

Carl was escorted back to his cell to finish writing up his version of events, and confession to the assault, with pen and paper in hand. Within five minutes, Wilbur, handcuffed, and shackled, was led to the interrogation room.

Entering the room with a Diet Coke, Billy Mac glared at Wilbur for at least 5 minutes, then began by asking, "Who paid you to do this? Carl gave me a story, and I hope he wasn't lying 'cause he laid everything on you."

Wilbur was about five feet eleven with long, greasy, stringy hair. He had a thin mustache that looked to be stained with chewing tobacco. He looked like a weasel.

"A man called me and said he wanted this black woman brought to this RV camp down on the river, the one down there behind the motel."

"What, man?"

"I don't know. The guy said he knew me and heard I done work like this. He would not give his name. His voice was departed or whatever, like Darth Vader in Star Trek."

"You mean distorted like he didn't want you to recognize him? And for your information, it's Star Wars."

"Yeah, that's it. The guy said he would pay all the money upfront. The money was hidden in a white bank bag behind some bushes at the old car dealership that closed in East Riverview. He described this lady to us and where she lived. He said the best thing to do would be to surprise her when she was leaving the house. He wanted us to bring her in her car."

"Wilbur, did you try to kill that woman? Carl said he thought you were going to."

"No, I got scared. I cut somebody once in a bar fight, but that's all. I was scared. I seen what she done to Carl! She's crazy!"

"You're sure you have no idea who this man may have been or how he heard about your line of work?"

"No, I have done collecting work for bookies, word sort of gets around, I guess. We just mainly threaten people, me, and Carl."

"Wilbur, have you had anybody in your family die lately?"

"Yeah, why would you ask that?"

"Hell, I don't know. Did you ever just do something and not know why you did it?"

"Yeah, but I didn't think you would. I've heard about you."

"Oh, you know me?"

"Most people have heard of you. You know from football and fighting and stuff, and say you're a badass."

"So, you heard that I'm a badass?"

"Yeah. You whipped Big Boy at the Royal lounge years back, and I was there."

Billy Mac leaned forward and motioned for Wilbur to lean in. Billy Mac whispered, "This is being recorded. So, I want this to be just between you and me. If you ever even think of trying to hurt that girl again, I'll torture you to death."

"Now back to the business at hand, and keep in mind, he who sings first gets the best deal. Now, who died, and where was the funeral?"

There was fear in Wilbur's eyes. He didn't know who would be worse, the girl or Billy Mac. "My Uncle Reni died about a month ago. The funeral was down there in the black part of town. It costs less."

"Benson Funeral Home?"

"Yeah, that's it."

Chapter 40

RV Park – Tracking Suspects

Billy Mac drove fast to the RV Park on the river; he was wasting no time. The manager's name tag read James Smith.

Pulling out his badge, Billy Mac repeated what the assailants said about JoAnn being brought to an RV at the Park. He told Mr. Smith that the RV was described as being off from the other RV's at the end of the Park.

"There was a man that rented an RV. We keep a couple on the property for that reason. He paid three months in advance in cash. When I asked him if he was vacationing, he told me he was renting it for the purpose of having private card games. He said there would be a little traffic in and out, but not that much."

"Is the RV still here?"

"Yes, I'll take you down there, and you can look inside."

"No, we need a search warrant to keep it legal, you know for the prosecution of the assailants. So just to be clear, you were paid in cash by this guy, and he did not give you a name, right?"

"That's right."

"Tell me what the man looked like, and anything he said that might help me identify him."

"He was about my height and weight, maybe a little heavier. I am five foot ten and one hundred eighty pounds. He may have been one ninety or two hundred. He had on a ball cap with Ford on it. It was white. His beard was sort of reddish and long, and he wore dark glasses. I had never seen him before."

"Then, he gave you no information about who he was or where he lived?"

"No, he wanted to keep it quiet, that's why he paid cash, and I didn't ask."

"Thank you, James, somebody will be back down here to search the RV. Don't let anyone touch or enter it."

Billy Mac called Langston and told him about the conversation. The sheriff told him that he had received a couple of calls from County Commissioners to include the Riverview Police Force in the investigation as a matter of courtesy and agency cooperation.

"You know Billy Mac, like me, these guys are elected, and they are politicians of sorts.

"Let me speak with Booley. I will request a couple of detectives I know on the force. I'll get back to you."

"Booley, this is Billy Mac. Can you send a couple of Riverview's finest to investigate something? The Sheriff and I want to include you in this investigation. This investigation is getting ugly; they have hurt JoAnn. I need the officers to search an RV here at the RV Park. If you took care of obtaining the search warrant, it would be helpful."

"That's terrible, is she alright? We would like to help Billy Mac. I'll get somebody on the case today. I'll and tell them to call you when they are done."

"Yes, she'll be fine. And thanks, Booley, sounds good," said Billy Mac.

He couldn't request anybody in particular. He would let Booley take care of that, or he would most likely get someone sub-par.

Billy Mac had two tracking devices, one to place on Hoss's car and one on Missy's car. He wanted one on Zora's car but only had two. He needed to figure out how to get devices on their cars without them knowing. He was going to call Pokey and get his advice. He could really use Pokey here now for his wisdom, expertise, and support.

He made the call to Pokey in Vegas and left a message as he was on his way home. He would check on JoAnn, then shower, and go to bed. He was dead tired.

As he was passing by the hair salon, he spotted Missy's car. She was in the back of the salon but would have a full view of her car through the window. He pulled in the driveway and left her a note on the windshield to call in case she saw him by her car. Then quickly and adeptly, he went to the back of the car, dropped down, and placed the magnet on the chassis close to the rear bumper.

Billy Mac decided to drive to the funeral home just in case he got lucky. There was Hoss's big Lincoln Navigator just sitting there waiting for him. There was a funeral, and the parking lot was full. Hoss must be in the back of the building as Billy Mac couldn't see him.

You will never get a better chance than this, he thought. In two minutes, the job was done. If anyone did see him, he would say he was in the area and was checking to see if Hoss was free. Wow! I'm getting lucky, he thought. He had a feeling they were moving fast toward solving a murder and a mystery.

On the way home, the Beach Boys sounded off; it was Pokey.

Billy Mac brought him up to date. "Golden Boy, if you need my help, then I'm on my way."

Billy Mac had just stepped out of the shower and was toweling off, getting ready to check on JoAnn when Missy called.

"Hello, Missy." Then he told her about JoAnn.

"My goodness, Billy Mac, that awful! I'm so glad you left that note to call you on my windshield. Who would do such a thing, and why?"

"My guess, whoever is behind the murder at the theater. As for why, because we are getting closer to solving the crime or crimes. And you can bet one thing Missy; we will solve this. Several people will be doing considerable time or maybe face the death penalty."

Missy sounded a little startled at what he said. "I have every confidence in you, Billy Mac. Is JoAnn at the hospital? I'd like to give her a call."

"Yes, I'm sure she would like that, and thank you, Missy, for your confidence in me. Now, if you'll excuse me, I need to call JoAnn and check on her. I wanted you to hear about the attempted abduction from me firsthand."

"I appreciate that, Goodnight Billy Mac."

Missy waited a bit and called JoAnn to check on her. She knew Billy Mac was calling her too.

Chapter 41

Hospital, Pokey, and Gene Lawrence

Billy Mac called JoAnn's phone, and she answered on the first ring.

"When is my man going to come rescue me? I'm bored. I don't like it here. I don't need to stay overnight, and I feel silly. It's not a life-threatening wound."

"It would be kidnapping. You know how hospitals are. You can't leave without a release. How are Mr. and Mrs. John Underwood holding up?"

"Somewhere between fair and great, they are greatly relieved, I'm fine. They left to go home a couple of hours ago. You get some rest. You have been working extremely hard. After you pick me up tomorrow, we can spend all day piecing this together."

"Definitely, I feel like you should stay with me for a while. It will be safer. Pokey is coming tomorrow to help."

"All right, you don't need to ask me twice to stay with you! I'm glad Pokey is coming; he will be a big help. Hey, I need to get someone to help me clean the house tomorrow, then he can stay at my house, seeing as it will be empty!"

"We'll talk tomorrow. I love you very much, JoAnn."

"I love you very much too, Billy Mac Logan."

# # # #

Check-Out

As usual, hospital check out time is on them, not the patient. After pleading, prodding, and throwing a minor fit, JoAnn was released at noon. Billy Mac took her by her house to pack some things to move to

Billy Mac's for her temporary stay. They had lunch on Billy Mac's deck, a couple of Jersey Mike's Subs.

"It would make me, and I'm sure your parents feel better if you were not involved at the moment with this investigation, at least in any recognizable form. I did not say that very well. Would you please just say what I mean?" Billy Mac said.

"My pleasure. I will continue my practice and furnish you with incomparable feedback and insight into the investigation, all while keeping a close watch on my lovely ass, avoiding any bullets or piercing objects that may find their way into it."

Billy Mac just shook his head and laughed. "Comfort me, you crazy ass woman, you scared the shit out of me."

JoAnn and Billy Mac called Pokey. He had landed in Birmingham, which was one hour away. He politely declined JoAnn's offer to stay at her home.

"JoAnn, you don't need an untidy old man like me, kicking around in your lovely home. I got to know those people at the Hampton Inn well on my last trip. I'm booked there, but it's so sweet of you to offer."

"I'm sure they will love to have you back at the Hampton, Pokey."

"This is a work trip. But y'all know old Pokey always has to have some fun. Have you told Tank and Bobbie Jean I'm coming?"

"No, I thought I would just let you surprise them."

"I'll do that, but tonight, I start my surveillance of Moyer Cutler Funeral Home, which just happens to be walking distance from the Hampton."

"Are you not coming by my house for dinner? I'm making spaghetti."

"Is about 6 o'clock okay, Billy Mac?"

"See you then."

As soon as he hung up, Billy Mac's phone rang. It was the private line of Detective Gene Lawrence with the Riverview Police department.

"Hey, Is that you, Gene?"

"Yep, it's your old crime-solving buddy. I heard you need my expert help."

"Man, I'm happy it's you. I would have asked for you, but you know I need to tread lightly with Booley. I sure don't miss the politics, Gene."

"I figured that. I had let Booley know earlier I would sure like to work on this case. My not so subtle way of saying, I want to solve crimes with Billy Mac Logan. I'm sure it pissed him off, but I think he is terrified not to cooperate."

"I wonder why you would say that. Gene, we have to make you Police Chief, a job you so deserve and get Booley kicked to the curb."

"Thank you, Billy Mac. I have some news for you of great interest. I'd rather do it in person. I learned that from my mentor, some guy named Billy Mac Logan."

"Can you come over to my house right now?"

"I'll be there in twenty minutes."

Upon arrival, Billy Mac introduced Gene to JoAnn. He explained their business and personal relationship. He made it clear that all confidences related to the case were shared with her, and he could feel comfortable speaking in front of her.

"What I am saying here has not been shared with our illustrious Police Chief. I do not trust him. We went to the RV Park, another detective and I, to search the RV. James Smith told us the same story he said he told you. An anonymous man, about five feet ten inches, two hundred pounds, comes down from Timbuktu or whatever pays cash three months in advance. Cash that was obviously hush money; Smith insisted that it is not against the law. This guy is most definitely covering his ass with this story, this James Smith. Billy Mac, do you know who owns the RV Park? I bet you do?"

"Okay, I'll bite. Hoss Hendricks owns the RV Park, and he owns Booley too."

"I knew you would know. James Smith is lying through his teeth, Billy Mac."

"Gene, so good to have you on this case and to be in contact with you again. I promise you that when this case is solved, I'll make sure your help is recognized and that we stay in touch. I have got some powerful people involved, and when it's over, Booley Lancaster will not remain Police Chief. That job should be yours. You know I'll help make that happen anyway I can."

"Thank you. It's always been my dream job. Just never counted on Booley ever leaving. He's firmly ensconced, or stuck!"

"Back to the RV Park. I don't guess anything much was found in the RV?"

"There were decks of cards, drinking glasses, and beer in the fridge. And also, a humidor with some fine cigars."

"All probably staged."

"Yes, most likely to corroborate the card story in case the authorities found out about the RV. We took fingerprints."

"I'll be keeping an eye on Mr. Hendricks. We will be having a nice discussion before long, he and I. Meanwhile, Gene, when I call, do I need to use this number?"

"Yes, it's my private line, Billy Mac."

Gene Lawrence left Billy Mac's home and made sure he was not followed.

Chapter 42

Spaghetti with Pokey

After Gene left, Billy Mac and JoAnn started to cook and get ready for their guest. While they were preparing, they talked.

"Something sinister has brewed and downloaded at Moyer Cutler, Billy Mac. I feel it so strongly."

"So, do I, Detective Underwood, and so does Pokey. That is one reason he did not accept your offer to stay at your house. I'll bet you he will want to keep a watchful eye on that place, and it is close to the Hampton Inn."

One hour later, Billy Mac's prized spaghetti sauce was done. It was seasoned just right with his secret ingredients he has now revealed to JoAnn. Just the right amount of garlic, onions, mushrooms, pimento, fresh cloves, and so on. He added a touch of Italian sausage to the breaded ground beef. Come on, Pokey, I'm hungry, Billy Mac said to himself.

The doorbell rang, Pokey handed a bottle of Cabernet Sauvignon to JoAnn and hugged her.

"JoAnn, it's good to lay these eyes on you again. Old Pokey has been worried about you. But I know you are one tough little lady."

"You're a sweet man, Pokey James."

"Pokey, I got some Chivas here. How about a pour?"

"Sounds inviting, with a splash of soda, if you have it."

"Got some in my little travel bar."

"Well, hello, Golden Boy!" Pokey addressed Billy Mac as he entered the room.

"I feel better already now that you're here. We got a big puzzle to solve."

"You just serve me up some of that spaghetti. That will give me the energy to get through the night. I'm going to be watching that old funeral home all night."

"Thought maybe that would be in your plans. Something evil is coming out of there."

"I already have a lead on that. I got lucky when I checked into the Hampton."

"How's that, Pokey?" asked JoAnn.

"Well, you know how I like to strike up conversations with people. First of all, I am a people person; and I just like people. JoAnn, I know in your line of work, counseling, you have probably experienced this. The more you get interested in someone and get them engaged, the more that they will reveal to you."

"Sure, it certainly works that way, at least the majority of the time."

"That fellow at the desk, Grisham was his first name, Grisham Garner. We started talking about what a clear night it was going to be. I told him I was working on this murder case with you guys and had come in from Las Vegas. His eyes lit up, and he started talking about how he was the curious type. He had always dreamed of being a private investigator. I told him I thought that was great. One of the key qualities of a good investigator was to be curious about everything and everybody. And you have to notice and think about things that most people don't. Grisham said that was him, curious.

For instance, he said, I work the night shift, and tonight is a big night. I asked him how so Grisham? He said every week, on this day, a jet comes streaming through the sky somewhere between 2 and 2:30 in the morning. It appears to land at the Riverview Airport. But what seems funny is that about that time, somebody leaves that funeral home and heads toward the airport. Now I know this because I take my smoke break in the back outside, and I can see the back of the funeral home from there."

I told him how that information is very interesting and observant. I asked him who covers the desk when you go out for a smoke. He held up his phone and said, my phone app. I usually take my tablet out there; I can see the whole lobby with all the cameras we got. Well, what do you think is going on, Grisham, I asked? I don't know he said, but it's like maybe somebody at the funeral home is meeting that jet.

"Are you thinking the same thing I am? You take the funeral home, and I'll take the airport."

"Man, JoAnn, that boy catches on fast. I'm not going to finish this drink, JoAnn, since I'm working tonight. I'm going to eat a little, well, maybe a lot, of spaghetti and take a nap, I'm tired, and this is going to be a long night."

"Let me get the food on the table. You guys have a seat in the dining room."

"You sure? You did just get out of the hospital, and I should be taking care of you."

"No worries, Billy Mac, I'm fine and can handle getting dinner on the table."

"Alright, you go ahead, I know better than to argue with you. Pokey and I need to make a call, and then we'll be in. I want us to have a couple of bulletproof vests."

"No need for the call Golden Boy, I brought two with me, the new soft kind the FBI uses. They say it will withstand an AK47."

Seated at the table, JoAnn served both men large portions of food. Garlic cheese bread, and fresh spring salad, covered with virgin olive oil and a splash of red wine vinegar.

JoAnn and Pokey decided not to open the wine. Pokey and Billy Mac were going to be working all night.

Chapter 43

The Funeral Home and the Jet

Pokey arrived for his surveillance sometime after midnight. He came equipped with night vision binoculars and a camera and set up where he could view the funeral home. At 2:15, two men exited the back door of Moyer Cutler Funeral Home. Pokey was in a thick hedged area along the southern boundary line of the funeral home's property. He was only about ten feet from the black Lincoln Navigator they were walking towards. He began taking pictures. The camera made no sound. The night vision goggles allowed him to view the two men; one was Hoss Hendricks, the owner of the funeral home. Pokey knew him from the murder scene at the party. The other man he had also seen at the party. He was dressed in uniform, Booley Lancaster, the Police Chief.

Pokey thought, well, I'll be damned. The two men entered the vehicle and waited briefly. Then Pokey saw the light in the sky traveling along the river, leaving a trail of emissions behind it. That must be the jet.

The car's engine sprung to life, and the men sped hastily out of the parking lot, carrying whatever they had put in the trunk of the vehicle.

Pokey called Billy Mac. "Two men just left the funeral home, with whatever they were carrying and put in the back of a black Navigator. The jet is on the way to the airport, and I spotted it flying by the river. I believe the men to be Hoss Hendricks and Booley Lancaster."

"I'm monitoring Hoss on my phone now. I have a GPS tracker on the Navigator and the app on my phone. It looks like they're heading my way."

"Be careful, Billy Mac. You got your vest on, don't you?"

"Yes, and I'm well hidden. There won't be a confrontation tonight. I'll get back to you, Pokey."

Billy Mac was in a good hiding spot, but with nothing but runway, it was hard to get as close as he would have liked. Billy Mac spotted the jet as it approached the runway. It landed beautifully. He loved the sound that a jet engine makes in the silence of the dark early morning. A man came out of the airport hangar with bright flashlights and directing apparatus. He was directing the jet where to park; the flashlights lit up the whole area. Billy Mac took a look through his binoculars and almost couldn't believe his eyes!

Whoa, he thought. Could it be? Yes, it was! The man was James Smith, the RV Park manager.

Only one man, the pilot, exited the plane. Billy Mac took pictures. He thought it was a Lear jet, but wasn't sure. He wasn't up on his jet models. He managed to get several good pictures of Hoss, Booley, James Smith, and the pilot.

Smith and the pilot loaded the contraband. They put it in the back seat of the pressurized cabin. The whole operation took less than five minutes; the plane did not refuel. The pilot took off quickly, flying east toward Atlanta.

Hoss and Booley spoke swiftly with Smith, then got in the Navigator and left. Billy Mac waited for Smith to go back inside, then he left at a jogging pace to go back to the jeep hidden with overgrowth behind the fence. Billy Mac cranked up and headed home. He called Pokey.

"Pokey, we hit pay dirt, man, what a lucky break. Sometimes I think you are not real!"

"Ha, ha, every man gets a horseshoe up his ass once in a while. As you know, that's the investigating business. But when something happens at a certain place, lots of times someone around that place has seen something. You just got to get it out of them. That's the skill; the rest is dumb luck."

"Sweet dreams Pokey, talk tomorrow."

"They would be sweeter if I had my Susan with me. Comfort of your woman, man, I'll see you tomorrow."

Chapter 44

Dream

JoAnn felt someone pinning her to the bed, and she could not move. Another man was waiting, laughing. She felt frozen in time. Had they drugged her?

The man lifted her up, put her on her feet. She was not gagged, shackled, or tied up. However, she could not move, not any part of her body. She was in a trance. Yes, they had to have drugged her. She should be fighting. Where was Billy Mac?

Come, the man said. You are one of us now. You will work for the dark side, like on Star Wars. You will be the devil's mistress. He said this as he grinned and showed fiery teeth.

JoAnn moaned loudly and began screaming.

"JoAnn, JoAnn! Wake up! You have been having a nightmare."

"Oh, Billy Mac! It was so real. Someone was trying to take me and make me the Devil's mistress."

"Let's get up for a minute and go in the den, and I'll get you a cold washcloth."

JoAnn only had a tee-shirt on, so she put on a pair of shorts and went to the sofa in the den. Billy Mac had on bike shorts. He added a tee-shirt. Then with cold water, wet a washcloth in the bathroom and went to the kitchen to get a solo cup full of cold water.

"Here, darlin', just a bad dream." Billy Mac wiped her forehead with the cold washcloth and handed her the water.

"Whew, that feels good. Silly dream, can't tell before breakfast."

"That's the rule, so I'll wait till morning. You know, JoAnn, I am not feeling right about getting you into all of this. It seems it has been another trauma piled on top of your health issues."

"As you and I discussed, I have backed off for now, on being overtly involved in the case. But I still want to help. Please understand, I enjoy this. I have always been interested in criminals, as you know. There is something exciting about crime investigation, especially how the criminal mind works Billy Mac. It's gotten in my blood. Plus, I know I can help you. If it gets to be too much for me, I'll let you know."

"I'm sold! I can't say this enough. You are one fascinating woman. Now, let me tell you what happened last night."

"As you know, Pokey found out from the night manager at the Hampton Inn that a jet flies into town every week and lands at the Riverview Airport in the wee hours of the morning. Someone from Moyer Cutler meets the plane and delivers some type of cargo. Last night the delivery boys were Hoss and Booley, and the night manager of the airport is none other than James Smith. The same James Smith that is the day manager at the RV Park where your assailants were going to take you. That park is owned by none other than Hoss."

"Wow, that's a good bit of information. Billy Mac, we will eventually figure all this out, especially if we keep getting big chunks of clues. Anyway, here's what I think. It is time to call the FBI. It seems like this operation could have international consequences, or it may be nothing. We have no proof of what they are doing. Maybe the bodies being desecrated are organ donors, although I'm sure they didn't know they would be, and being sold on the black market. At the very least, it's getting dangerous, has crossed state lines, and I have a strong feeling we should call Holderfield."

"Okay, I agree. I think, as a courtesy to Langston, you should call him also."

"There is no time like the present."

Sheriff Langston answered on the first ring. JoAnn announced the call as urgent, apologized for the hour, and asked if he had time now to listen. The Sheriff responded affirmatively and listened intently as JoAnn relayed the facts as they knew them so far. She talked for 20 minutes with no interruption and ended by saying she strongly believed that Marvin Holderfield would want this information. She felt a dire need to call him.

What an intelligent lady, thought Billy Mac. She never ceases to amaze me. I love her to death.

JoAnn was extraordinarily articulate and poignant in her presentation. The manner in which she told the story and asked for permission would have made it impossible for the Sheriff to refuse her request.

Sheriff Langston didn't fall off the collard truck yesterday. He treasured JoAnn's relationship with the FBI. That could be to his advantage in the future, and he knew he could call her to intervene on his behalf.

The Sheriff asked if they minded having a conference call with Marvin. JoAnn replied no, but insisted that it must be made on the encrypted line she had. She asked if he could come to Billy Mac's home to make the call with them. He said he would be right over.

FBI Agent Marvin Holderfield responded to JoAnn's call by saying, "Thanks for the call. This information is top secret. Any of you three should not share it with anyone. Agent Elizabeth Duke and I will fly into Birmingham, Alabama, either tomorrow or the next day. I cannot overemphasize the importance of this matter. Please keep your calendars clear for the next few days.

"Sheriff, how about a drink?"

Sheriff Langston told himself that he was now off duty. Brian said out loud. "JoAnn, could you make it a double?"

"Coming right up."

Chapter 45

JoAnn and Billy Mac

After the Sheriff left, Billy Mac checked his tracking devices on the tablet. There was Missy Hendricks' Lexus in Mount Cheaha. That was where Missy suggested they first meet to discuss surveillance of Hoss. Hoss's car was at the Moyer Cutler Funeral Home, where it stayed most of the time. Very interesting.

"JoAnn, when was the last time you spoke with Amanda?"

"Maybe a week ago. She says she spends a lot of time at the Bank. Without coming out and saying it, she indicated that several things needed to be changed that Greg had implemented. I asked her if she got involved much in the funeral business, and she said no. She said it was too macabre for her; she left that to Hoss and put all of her efforts in improving the bank and bolstering the bottom line."

"What is your current opinion of Amanda?"

"Billy, I don't know anymore. I haven't spent any time with her since before the party. She appears to be a workaholic. She may be right in the thick of this alongside Hoss. As far as we know, it was her idea to switch places with her husband. Who knows?"

"The Shadow?"

"You remind me so much of Tank. Damn, you guys are clever!"

"I'm sure the FBI guys will be crazy about me."

"Oh, of course, that goes without saying. What was your name again?"

"You know what wouldn't be so pleasant?"

"You mean if the agent didn't bathe?"

"Worse than that. What if Sheriff Langston was secretly married to Booley Lancaster, and they were in cahoots?"

"Have you started drinking again? Maybe you got a stash of weed I don't know about?"

"No, just getting a little giddy from all of this. It's pretty hard to believe. No telling what we will hear from Agents Holderfield and Duke."

"I wonder if the agents are going to allow Pokey and Gene Laurence in on this."

"You heard how emphatically he told us to keep it down home, as you and Tank would say."

"I need to put trackers on Zora Benson and Amanda's cars. That may be tricky."

"Why don't you teach me how to do that?"

"Because it's too dangerous, maybe another time. I'm just too nervous about you right now. You could, however, play a part in flushing them out."

"Billy Mac, if they are involved, they may be highly suspicious of what we know, which could spell trouble. I say we wait and discuss this with the Agents."

"Okay, I believe you are right. Anyway, I want to see if Pokey can find out anything about why Missy is in Cheaha. Hopefully, you and I can get our minds off this for the next twenty-four hours if that's possible."

"Oh, I believe I know a way that will work for at least a few hours."

Chapter 46

Pokey at Cheaha

Pokey received the call from Billy Mac, who passed on the information about Missy's odd location. Pokey went by to get Billy Mac's tablet that was synchronized with the tracking device on Missy's car.

Pokey left Billy Mac's house and headed for Cheaha. Upon arrival at Cheaha, Pokey was able to locate the cabin where Missy was staying. Her Lexus was parked outside, but no other cars were in sight. The cabin was close to a hiking trail. However, there did not appear to be a very strategic location for him to hide.

It's a good thing he had planned to disguise himself with a well-built nose and glasses and a beret. Also, he had brought a wheelchair. He did not want to take a chance on being recognized by someone. The location of the cabin forced a change of plans. But for now, he would improvise.

He took some pictures of the cabin and Missy's car. Somehow, he needed to flush her out of the cabin. If he could do that, and wait until she was gone, he could plant a listening device and camera inside the cabin.

Pokey went up to the parking lot and put on his disguise. He got the wheelchair out and motored on down the hiking trail.

When he got to the little path leading off to the cabin, he parked there. Shortly some hikers approached. They appeared to be two couples.

Perfect, he thought. "Excuse me," he pleaded from his wheelchair, in a perfect Irish accent, "I'm having a bit of a problem. I have congestive heart failure, and I have become overheated and can't catch my breath. Could you help me just a second, please?"

"Of course," a girl replied, "Will some bottled water help?"

"Yes, but I need to get inside a minute, out of the heat. Could you help me get down to that cabin? Do you mind knocking on the door and asking if I could come in for a few minutes?"

Both men jogged down to the cabin, which was only about one hundred fifty feet from them.

Missy answered the door. Pokey could see from there it was her. The men jogged back and said to come on. Pokey motored down with the two girls walking beside him. There was a handicap ramp up to the porch, and Missy opened the door for him to enter.

Pokey kept his head down with his collar turned up; he had dark glasses and a prominent nose. He was unrecognizable, even to someone who knew him well.

He spoke, continuing to use a thick Irish accent. "Thank you, Miss. This cool air will save me. I'll be gone in just a few minutes."

"Take your time. I'm leaving shortly. Just stay until then. Can I get you some water?"

"Sure. Thank you, kids, go on about your business. I'll be fine. I don't want to be a burden to ya. All I needed was this cool air. I'm so grateful to you, dear ones. Go now, get back to walkin'."

"Okay, if you're sure," said the girl who appeared to be the leader. They went to tell Missy, who was in the kitchen, they were leaving. One of the couples offered to stay with Pokey while they went to speak with Missy.

"I suppose he is not a serial killer, and he seems genuine."

"Maybe we should stay," one of the boys said.

"Oh no, I'm okay."

Pokey sensed what was going on and said, "As soon as I get me water, I'll be leavin'."

When Missy and the other couple entered the room, the other couple stated, "He says he is okay. He'll go ahead and leave when he drinks his water and cools down."

"Y'all go. He probably needs to sit a minute or two, and after all, he is in a wheelchair."

The couples took advantage of the opportunity and left.

"Miss, I don't want to be a burden. A load of thanks from Shaun Kelly Dowling. I think I just needed out of the sun, bad ticker," as he patted his heart.

"You sit here. I'll be just a few minutes packing, and then we can leave together. I can help you to your car."

"Oh, lovely, thanks, my dear."

As Missy shut the door to her bedroom, Pokey made his move. The only place anyone could meet was in this large room. Pokey jumped out of the chair and quickly put a listening device in the flue of the giant stone fireplace. Then he tiptoed to the other end of the room, stood on a dining room chair, and put a camera, well hidden, in the chandelier. It would be facing the den furniture.

Pokey guzzled his bottle of water, wrote a quick note saying, "To my angel in the woods. My deepest gratitude for your kindness to this old man, Mr. Dowling, I don't want to be a burden, so I'm off; I'll be fine on me own. He put a $100 bill on top of the note and left it under the water bottle. Pokey then quickly motored out. He did not feel like he should spend any more time with Missy for fear of discovery.

When Pokey got to the car, he said to himself, thank you, Lord, for making me so lucky in my work and so good at disguises. We need to catch some bad people.

Pokey called Billy Mac, "Hey, you remember that movie "Unforgiven" Billy Mac?"

"One of my favorites, seen it three or four times."

"Well, you remember that part when William Mooney told that writer that he had always been lucky in killing?"

"Yeah, I think that was after he killed Little Bill and all those men in the saloon."

"Some of us are lucky in different ways. I have always been lucky, as you know, in taking risks in the detective business, especially when I go undercover."

"Yeah, I'll certainly vouch for that."

"Today, I pulled off one of my all-time best." Pokey proceeded to tell him the whole story.

"Sometimes, I wonder if you're from this planet. Are you going to bring the monitoring devices over here?"

"On my way."

Billy Mac and Pokey discussed their next move and decided to track Amanda. Pokey had all the details he needed, her home, her car, and her workplace. Pokey then headed back to the Hampton Inn to rest.

The rest of the day, JoAnn and Billy Mac spent relaxing. Tomorrow was big. The FBI was coming to town.

Chapter 47

Meeting with the FBI

Marvin Holderfield and Elizabeth Duke came up the walk and knocked on the door. Their meeting was at JoAnn's house. She and Billy Mac felt it would be more comfortable being in her own home; they wanted to keep her involvement under wraps. Also, she could show them the garage where the attempted abduction went down.

Agent Holderfield was about six feet tall and one hundred ninety pounds. His head was shaven, and he had black eyebrows over dark brown eyes. Marvin sported black cowboy boots, jeans with a wide black belt, and a black tee top. His complexion was dark, and he had the whitest teeth.

Elizabeth Duke had short red hair, cut into a pageboy, a spattering of freckles, and big green eyes. She had on dark brown leggings, a Stanford University white tee with red letters, the same one JoAnn owned, and she donned low heeled brown Sperry's.

Curiously, Agent Duke and JoAnn were dressed similarly.

Greetings were exchanged, and Marvin began, "JoAnn, I brought one of the Bureaus upcoming bright stars from your Alma Mater, Agent Elizabeth Duke."

"Hi, it looks like you are wearing my shirt Elizabeth. I love my Stanford tee."

"Love mine too. I am proud of my education there, Computer Science. How about you, JoAnn?"

"A Doctorate in Behavioral Neuroscience, with an undergrad in Psychology from Birmingham Southern."

"Since no one asked, I just went to little 'ole Texas and studied criminology. But I wanted to be in the Bureau since grade school."

"I spent two years at Auburn University then finished in Criminal Justice at Jacksonville State University."

"Billy Mac, I hear you were an extraordinary, even legendary athlete," said Marvin.

"I love sports. Unfortunately, a two hundred seventy-pound defensive linemen from Mississippi State ended my quarterbacking and all sports for me in my sophomore year at Auburn. It was a cheap shot, side of the knee after the whistle. I left school after that; I was there on a full-ride athletic scholarship. Later, two years later, in fact, that man drove from Mississippi to Riverview, knocked on my door, and tearfully apologized to me. That was my first real lesson in forgiveness, and it was not an easy one. Afterward, we became friends. Three years ago, I was a pallbearer at his funeral.

One valuable lesson I learned from sports was we never know what life is going to throw at us. As my 'ole buddy Tank Wilson says, do the best you can and let the rough end drag. Don't ask me what that means because I'm not quite sure."

Marvin grinned. "When JoAnn called, she briefed me on the case regarding your discovery and the events to date. We are not only here today for this case, but also because Elizabeth has been working for two years on a case classified as top secret. We feel it may be related. As JoAnn revealed your findings to me, it sounds likely. Before we let Elizabeth brief us on that, JoAnn, why don't you and Billy Mac tell us the story from the beginning to date, what you know and who you suspect."

JoAnn began: "A group we belong to that we call the "POETS," Phooey on Everything Tomorrow's Saturday, planned a big party to be held at an old renovated movie theater called the Pitman in downtown

Riverview. The old theater seats have been gutted so tables and chairs can provide the seating; the idea is to have a dinner theater. The stage now has an overhead crane to help move and load sets needed for stage plays. The party, called Friends Faceoff, took place on May 2nd. It began with cocktails and food from 6 to 7 o'clock. Then there was a brief program from 7 to 7:15. Billy Mac spoke first. Then as Greg Sistern, owner of the Riverview Bank and sponsor of the event, began speaking, a body fell from the roof over the stage area, seemingly from out of nowhere. Here is what we suspect, Billy Mac?"

"Just as JoAnn said, the body fell from overhead. One leg was tied to a cable. When the body fell, it swung back and forth like a pendulum; it eventually became still. We suspect the victim was murdered Friday, May 1st. The body was then brought to the theater sometime during the night. Someone placed it on the overhead crane tracts in such a position that a hand-held device could trigger the body's release by someone at the event.

Whoever murdered this man wanted everyone to know by staging a very public display. The body was identified as Jeffrey Thomas by me, the Mother of his child, and a picture sent to his Aunt in Cleveland, Ohio. The reason I was able to identify the body was two-fold. One, he was wearing a shirt that had slipped down around his neck, revealing a bare upper torso. Jeff had an appendix scar from childhood. I saw what I thought to be that scar on the body. Second, I saw his face, which appeared to be Jeff. I had just had lunch with him two days prior. However, I did not get a real close look.

In retrospect, it was a hasty ID in the heat of the moment. I have a strong gut feeling that might not have been Jeff Thomas. Once my head cleared, I remembered more detail. The skin on the face was a different tone from what I remembered of Jeff's, and it was also fresher. It had not yet turned the slightly greenish grayish tone of the torso. I am also suspicious of how quickly they removed the body from a crime scene.

They would not allow me to see the body again, orders from Booley Lancaster, Chief of Police. We believe he is involved in this sinister business in some capacity, but I'll address that later.

I then asked myself, 'Who was the victim if not Jeff Thomas? JoAnn and I think it may be David Dingler, Jeff Thomas' partner. They lived together behind Jeff's Aunt's home in Shaker Heights, which is in Cleveland, Ohio. JoAnn and I suspect that Jeff Thomas set this whole murder up to make people think he was dead, but we're not sure why. According to his aunt, he had a lot of enemies. We suspect that he handpicked David Dingler months ago to be his fall guy. David Dingler was David Castilla and originally from Cuba. He and Jeff looked like brothers. They both had hazel eyes, were about the same height and weight, and had the same olive skin tone, despite David being Cuban and Jeff being Italian on his father's side. There was one glaring difference. David was about twenty years younger and did not have grey in his hair like Jeff. But at a quick glance, and from far away, it looked like Jeff. The murderer could also have used makeup and hair dye to make the body appear older. JoAnn, you want to tell them about Anna and Cortez?"

"Sure. The first thing we did was go to Shaker Heights to visit Jeff's Aunt Sophie after the murder. As Billy Mac has mentioned, Jeff has a rich widowed Aunt that owns the guest house where Jeff and David lived together as a couple. Aunt Sophie insisted we spend the night, said she loves to have guests. In the process of searching the guest house, I found some letters from Anna, who turned out to be Jeff's sister. Anna is somewhere near twenty years younger than Jeff. She has been diagnosed as a paranoid schizophrenic and resides in a Clinic called Lanier Clinic in Cleveland, Ohio.

During our conversation, Anna told us that Jeff had called her yesterday from Riverview, which would have been the day after his body was discovered. When we left the facility, we asked Dr. Hargrove about this. He said they had taken Anna's phone away. However, Anna, unbeknownst to Dr. Hargrove, has a hidden cell phone in her room. She has since called and told us about receiving a call from Jeff. Anna had asked for my card when we left, so she has my phone number. When I asked her if she was sure about the call being from Jeff, she said yes. She knew his voice, and they had a secret code word "virgin" that he always said when he called."

JoAnn then proceeded to tell Marvin and Elizabeth about Cortez and how he seemed to be fearful for his life. She told them that Cortez had called Tank about wanting to work full time at the butcher shop. JoAnn relayed that Tank said he was by far the best person he had ever seen with a knife. Then she dropped the bombshell.

His friend, Eduardo, told us they were forcing Cortez to mutilate and desecrate bodies. The interview was in Spanish, in which I am fluent. Eduardo said Cortez thought God would punish him if the bosses didn't get him first. When I asked him specifically what Cortez was doing to the bodies, he almost screamed: Tara cortado, Tara Cortado, as he outlined his face."

Elizabeth spoke firmly, "Cut off face, cut off face, cut off face!"

"Exactly," said Joann. "Weird, right? Then, Cortez disappears, and suddenly reappears."

Billy Mac continued where JoAnn left off. "We believe Cortez worked for them under duress. And before reappearing, they spoke with his wife, and they were most likely both threatened with repercussions if Cortez left or talked. We know from speaking with his kids that his wife was summoned to the funeral home by Hoss Hendricks, telling her he would help find Cortez. Chalk that up as another "suspect" that you asked about. I'm quite sure they threatened to harm his family,"

JoAnn and Billy Mac continued to relate the story of Cortez. Their visit to his home before and after he was reunited with his family. They were sure to relay how odd Cortez and his wife acted.

For another two hours, the couple continued to present and talk about the case with Agents Holderfield and Duke. They covered JoAnn's attempted abduction through to Amanda being the biological daughter of Missy and Jeff, and of course, the delivery to the jet at the airport.

Billy Mac also spoke about his suspicions regarding the involvement of Zora Benson, Hoss Hendricks, the Sistern's, possibly Missy Hendricks, and Jeff Thomas (if he was still alive), in illegal activity involving both funeral homes. He believed they were using Riverview bank, which Greg and Amanda own, in an attempt to hide the large sums of money they were making.

"Whew, let's take a break, that's a lot of information to digest," exclaimed Marvin.

JoAnn brought out some finger sandwiches and iced tea. Marvin took a pimento cheese, Elizabeth took two chicken salads. Billy Mac took two of each.

The group had a friendly conversation getting to know each other, leaving the discussion of the case until after they ate. Both Marvin and Elizabeth worked out of the Atlanta Field Office. Marvin was just named Special Agent in charge of the Atlanta Office. Billy Mac and JoAnn knew this case had to be important. They were talking to the top man in the office. JoAnn had made a friend in a high place, and Marvin also projected his confidence in Elizabeth Duke.

Marvin spoke, "Billy Mac, over the years, I have gained a lot of respect for private investigators. The great ones all share information. I have a friend with thirty years with the Bureau. When he retired, he became a private investigator. I have learned so much from him. By the way, you have done a remarkable job on this case. It's amazing how far you have come in such a short period of time."

"Thank you. I have had cooperation from the Sheriff and one of the detectives I know on the Riverview Police Force. Also, a top-notch investigator named Pokey James from Las Vegas has been invaluable. Is there a possibility we could share some, or all, of this information with them? They've been working alongside us from the beginning."

"Yes, that is a possibility. We have a need to know provision."

"In particular, it would be beneficial to include Sheriff Langston and Pokey James, and not the Chief of Police. We believe he is involved in the seedy side of this. So, you make that call, I'm close to them and don't want to involve anyone just based on friendship."

"Elizabeth, what do you think?" asked Marvin.

"Why don't I give the background on what we have been investigating, then we can make a decision."

"The floor is open, Elizabeth, if you are ready to give your briefing."

Agent Elizabeth Duke's Briefing:

"For almost two years now the Bureau has been investigating an immoral, sordid, illegal business aiding some of the most sought-after criminals to lose their identity. This is being accomplished by hiding their most identifiable feature, their face. With the development of facial recognition software, changing your face is imperative to not being caught, especially for the more high-profile criminals.

Surgeons can now perform a procedure to remove the face of a person that was recently declared clinically dead. Clinical death is a medical term for the cessation of blood circulation and breathing. The skin can remain alive up to twelve hours with the aid of available machines. We think there are three locations in the United States where skin, facial skin, is being grafted from a corpse to a live person. Presently this procedure only benefits criminals. To our knowledge, this technology has not been approved to be used for humanitarian purposes and thus is an illegal medical procedure. We believe the locations for these operations are Los Angeles, Chicago, and Atlanta.

As for the investigation in Riverview, a jet could be in Atlanta in twenty minutes. It makes sense the funeral homes here may be supplying the faces. We have discovered that this procedure can cost the recipient as much as $500,000. Of course, this figure is not exact, it could be more, and it could be less. What we are sure of is it is very lucrative. We also have reason to believe this is not just happening in our country, but overseas as well.

What you two and others have accomplished here has brought us closer than we have ever been able to get in solving these heinous crimes. We also believe they are selling organs on the black market. However, at this time, we don't have enough evidence to prove it. We believe organs have been extracted from the bodies without permission and put on the black market for sale, even poop!"

"Poop?" asked JoAnn.

"There are lots of good bacteria in poop, and yes, it has been sold on the black market, though I don't personally know the purpose it serves. However, the real crime is body desecration, aiding and abetting criminals, illegal medical procedures, and the selling of organs on the black market. In the Riverview case, murder is now added to the mix. Any questions?"

"How long have these facial transplants been going on?" asked JoAnn.

"Possibly as long as twenty years," answered Elizabeth.

"I'm a little stunned, but I'm not surprised, medicine can do many things that are not approved," said JoAnn. "Aside from that, Billy Mac has been suspicious of the funeral homes here for a while now."

"The best evidence we could obtain to put this ring out of business would be to confiscate the cargo that is going to the jet. We need constant surveillance on the airport and both funeral homes," said Marvin.

"Billy Mac, about this murder. Do you have any suspects or motives? Also, do you suspect anyone else who may be involved?"

"We have reason to believe Jeff Thomas killed David Dingler, AKA David Castro. He wanted it to be a public display, so there would be no doubt that he was dead. Including his nemesis, The Federal Bureau of Investigation. Whatever he was into, he didn't want y'all digging into it. Also, Jeff has always been the showman. He wanted to be on the grand stage. JoAnn and I have discussed at length who we think was involved. But we can't be sure, just speculation. Of course, we have no doubts that Jeff was the instigator and planned his own murder.

We also now have reason to believe that Hoss Hendricks knew about it and was involved to some degree. Amanda Sistern is possibly involved. She has taken over Riverview Bank rather suddenly. As Jeff's daughter, JoAnn believes she possibly inherited his sociopathic and psychopathic personality. It's also possible Zora Benson knew about this whole business and may also have a hand in the pot. We are not sure about Missy Hendricks. JoAnn suspects her more than I do, but she has little reason to be involved as far as I can see. We both doubt the involvement of Greg Sistern in the murder per se. However, he is still a suspect as he was complicit in hiding the large sums passing through the bank. As to the why, and how, all this may have gotten started, I would like to defer to JoAnn."

"Jeff Thomas is very likely a sociopath or psychopath and has some tendencies of a serial killer. He tortured animals, set fires, and was a bedwetter as a child. All this we know courtesy of Billy Mac as they were childhood friends. Therefore, he fits the Triad. His daughter Amanda is gracious and engaging. However, I do not know if she is very compassionate; she is cold, almost emotionless. Hoss Hendricks and Zora Benson seem to be the same way, and nothing seems to rattle them. Missy Hendricks is an outstanding actress, in my opinion. It is strange that Amanda, the daughter of Missy, and her husband Greg just happened to come to Riverview, as Billy Mac pointed out at the beginning of our investigation. Why would they come to Riverview from such lucrative surroundings in Texas and buy an interest in a funeral home and a bank in a small town, which just happened to be 20 years ago? Just a theory, but I believe they may have met on a website for sociopaths on the dark web. The web site they were on connected with the doctors on the front lines. From there, they concocted this very lucrative scheme."

"All this is very interesting. JoAnn and Billy Mac, of all the suspects, who do you think would be the easiest to crack and to turn on the others?" asked Marvin.

JoAnn looked to Billy Mac to respond. Billy Mac said, "The ones who weren't involved with the murder directly, such as Greg and Zora. If they don't crack, I'm sure others will. That is where your expertise shines. Isn't that right, Marvin?"

"We will make a deal, to solve this mystery and crack this ring wide open. It is far-reaching, though, to shut down the whole ring. For that to happen, this group would have to know all the players. I'm sure whoever heads up the ring has been cautious."

"I do suspect Hoss Hendricks might be involved in the murder, and I think he knows more about this ring than anybody. He's probably the ring leader in Riverview. Additionally, I have the feeling that he could be the best whistleblower if it would help his cause. He is out for himself and cares not a bit for anyone else," said JoAnn.

"I agree," said Billy Mac.

"Then, he is our target. Let's set a time to have the other's over to share our information," continued Marvin.

"We will do it today if you want," said Billy Mac.

'Okay, this evening then, here, at 7 o'clock," stated Marvin.

"I'll get to work on setting it up it right away," said JoAnn

"Ditto," said Billy Mac.

"Unless we hear from you guys, we will see you at seven," said Marvin.

"The agents left, and JoAnn and Billy Mac started making calls.

"What about Steve Sanders," said JoAnn, "Doesn't he need to be in on this?"

"Yes, I forgot him. Call Marvin to be sure about including him."

JoAnn called Marvin and quickly got approval, then called Sheriff Langston and Steve Sanders and expressed the urgency of the meeting. Both men said they would attend.

Billy Mac called Pokey, who was very excited. He said he had worked with the LA offices of the Bureau and knew several people there. Billy Mac wondered if he should have brought up Booley as someone who may crack, but he purposely did not. It may be selfish, he thought, but I want him myself. As far as Gene Lawrence, the Riverview detective was concerned, there would be a time to bring him in. But he did not feel as if now was that time.

Billy Mac also discussed the planting of the devices with Pokey. That could be viewed as 'food of the poison vine' as legal terms go. A good defense lawyer could introduce a motion to preclude. Therefore, the evidence would be inadmissible, as it was obtained illegally. Pokey agreed they would not mention that unless push came to shove.

Chapter 48

The FBI, Sheriff, DA, and Pokey

The meeting with the Sheriff, District Attorney, and Pokey was going well and into its second hour. Marvin knew some of the persons in the Los Angeles office that Pokey had worked with previously. This seemed to ease Marvin's mind, and it made sharing the top-secret information more palatable.

Marvin was planning to have an undercover agent fly into the Riverview Airport on the pretense of having a meeting with a local business. As the group was trying to figure out who that might be, JoAnn offered a suggestion.

"Do you have agents familiar with real estate and property development?" asked JoAnn.

"Yes, we do, and thank you, that would be a perfect cover. They could be looking for land, and would not have to be specific about anything," said Marvin.

"We are starting a Sheriff's sale soon on some foreclosed properties if you needed to use that," said Langston.

"Yes, that would be something tangible and should not cast suspicion. We can have one or two agents on surveillance at the airport beginning immediately every night. Sheriff Langston, what is your suggestion for surveillance of the funeral home?" asked Marvin.

Before the Sheriff could answer, Pokey said, "I got the funeral home if you want. Billy Mac, what do you want to do?"

"That depends on what Marvin decides. There are four people we need to follow. Hoss Hendricks, Missy Hendricks, Amanda Sistern, and Zora Benson. Those are the ones JoAnn and I suspect having involvement in the murder. There are tracking devices on Hoss and Missy's cars. I wasn't going to mention this for fear of its inadmissibility in court. Still, as they are already in place, it will allow us to follow them at a distance."

"We will put agents on each of the four," said Marvin.

"Great, then I will keep an eye on our police chief, Booley Lancaster," said Billy Mac.

"Sounds like we got a plan. We each need a prepaid phone. We don't want to use our personal lines. Elizabeth and I will get them to you soon. I'll have them preloaded with everyone's respective numbers," Marvin said.

It was 11 o'clock when the next to the last of the group got up to leave. Marvin and Elizabeth departed immediately after.

Billy Mac and Pokey had decided to tell Marvin and Elizabeth about the implant of the surveillance devices in the Cheaha Cabin as well. This eased Billy Mac's conscience. Marvin laughed when Pokey told the story, then looked at Pokey and said, "Good work."

"An exhausting but exciting day," said JoAnn.

"Yes, I feel good about how things are progressing. I just hope the jet comes this week. Let's go to bed, tomorrow's gonna be another busy day," said Billy Mac.

Chapter 49

The Next Morning – Billy Mac and JoAnn

"Billy Mac, only about three percent of men, are sociopathic, and only about one percent of women. That makes it difficult for the other ninety-seven percent of us to understand them, even doctors, the human mind is complex.

We do know they know right from wrong, but they never see or admit their wrongdoing. They have no conscience or remorse. Interviews with people on death row have determined this. They view people with a conscience as weak. Sociopaths are experts at reading people through body language. They will go to any lengths to get their way and are narcissistic. They love being in charge. A guy like Jeff Thomas may know you are smarter than he is, but he thinks he has an advantage over you because you have a sense of morality. You have a conscience!"

"If he is alive, which we suspect, catching him and putting him away is a priority. I have a feeling we are getting very close."

They finished their breakfast, and by then, the beeper was going off on Billy Mac's tracking device at the Cheaha cabin.

The camera device was not working, but the audio was.

A female voice spoke, "We have to take care of him. He needs to disappear."

"How could we even justify that?" another female voice spoke.

"Why would we have to justify it?" said a male voice, "He would just disappear. We have the best disposal system in the world. Any remaining bones ashes don't have any traceable DNA. It would suit me if we could get rid of that black girl, too, while we're at it."

"No," said the second female voice. "Absolutely no! Too risky!"

"I agree," said the other female. "Too much suspicion if they disappear at the same time. Maybe we should just leave things alone for a while. You know, let the dust settle."

"We can decide later. We need to get out of here for a while," said the female.

Billy Mac and JoAnn had been listening intently.

JoAnn spoke, "We need to call Holderfield and Duke now to fill them in on this conversation."

"Yes, and we also need legal authority to access those devices."

The call was placed to Marvin, and Billy Mac told him what happened and identified the voices. He told Marvin he had the recording.

Marvin placed a call to the Attorney General of Alabama. He requested participation in the conversation as the commander of the Alabama Bureau of Investigation.

Arrangements were made to gain access to the cabin immediately. Pokey James was asked to participate since he knew the whereabouts of the devices. Within an hour, the residents of the cabin had dispersed. Shortly after, men wearing termite control uniforms entered the cabin; one was Pokey. Pokey found the audio in the chimney just as he left it. The camera in the chandelier had a defective battery and was replaced. Marvin now had warrants giving law enforcement the required legal authority to monitor the cabin.

While searching the cabin, the crew discovered a section of the floor in the back had been reconstructed. It could be lifted so that one could drop to the crawl space. There was no back door to the cabin. According to the State Authorities that ran the Park, the trap door must have been created by the renters. A rug was thrown over it to hide the door.

"What is your best guess, Billy Mac? Who are the targets the group was talking about?" asked Marvin.

"Hoss Hendricks and Zora Benson."

"JoAnn?"

"I concur, maybe, yes, I suppose it could be Billy Mac and me. However, getting rid of those two would greatly increase their profits."

"We are moving immediately to arrest Zora Benson and Hoss Hendricks, sudden change!!"

Chapter 50

The Arrests

"Get the warrants ready. I would like for Elizabeth, Billy Mac, the Sheriff, and me to make the arrest. Let's go," said Marvin.

The foursome charged into Benson Funeral Home. Zora was in a meeting with her employees. It abruptly ended when Marvin and Elizabeth showed their badges and asked for everyone, except Zora, to leave the room immediately.

Zora was read her Miranda Rights and placed under arrest and was immediately carted to the County Jail in handcuffs. She was then taken to the interrogation room, offered a glass of water, and told they would get back to her. She was extremely distraught and tearful as Billy Mac viewed her through the video surveillance. It was a typical play by law enforcement to let the suspect sweat for a while before interrogation.

The next stop was to arrest Hoss Hendricks. The group barged into his office, where he was taking his usual afternoon thirty-minute nap on his big leather sofa.

Hoss was surprised! He was read his rights, and ten minutes later, he was in an interrogation room.

Marvin suggested that Billy Mac and Sheriff Langston take Zora, and he and Elizabeth would question Hoss.

Zora was a mess, a very emotional mess, and Billy Mac believed she was not faking it. He asked that she be uncuffed and handed her a bottle of water.

Billy Mac's instincts were guiding him. His approach was sincere but a little manufactured as well. He began his interrogation with a prayer, asked for forgiveness for Zora, and the healing of her soul. Brian went along with Billy Mac. They had decided Brian would listen, looking stern, and Billy Mac do the questioning.

"Zora, do you have any idea how serious the charges against you are?" asked Billy Mac.

"I swear to God Billy Mac, I did not know anything about the murder, or whatever that body falling out of the top of the stage was. I'll take a lie detector test. I would not have anything to do with killing anybody!"

"Zora, tell us the whole story. I believe you didn't know about the murder. My partner here is not as sure. You can help yourself by cooperating. Start at the beginning,"

"Twenty years ago, I met Hoss Hendricks and Jeff Thomas at a National Funeral Directors Convention, the NFDA. Somehow they knew I was buying Williams Funeral Home in Riverview. They told me they could bolster my sales, for lack of a better word, and send me some business on the embalming side. It would be a profitable venture for me, they said. What they wanted in return was for me to send them cremations. I was young, ambitious, and eager to make money. Uncle Stoney thought it was a good idea as well. After all, he was putting up the money, so it was partly his decision."

"You did know what was going on over there, didn't you, Zora?"

"Not for the first few years. Not until I found out what Cortez Cortez was doing. That was about ten years ago. Oh, I suspected they were selling organs. That has always been a profitable business, but then I learned about the "faceoffs." That's what they were calling them, "faceoffs." Sometimes they called it the Skin Game. I was eventually told the faces were being used to hide a criminal's identity by implanting them with a new face. They wanted me to know, so in case I got a conscience, I would be fearful of incriminating myself. I was paid well for my silence."

"Are you aware of the jet that flies the skin and organs out of here?" asked Billy Mac.

"Yes. That is all handled at Moyer Cutler. We just sent a black man over for cremation. I suspect whatever they farm from him will go out on the next jet, probably in a couple of days."

Brian spoke, "We can recommend to the FBI if you continue to cooperate fully, that charges be reduced or even dropped against you, full immunity."

"Meanwhile, your life could be in danger. They're bound to know you've been arrested. We will keep you under surveillance at a safe house." said Billy Mac. "I suspect the FBI will be talking with you soon."

"Thank you, and I will tell them everything I know, I swear. A woman my age wouldn't survive in jail, and I'm not going there for any of them."

"Who gave you the money to have Cortez followed?" asked Billy Mac.

"It was Hoss. I wasn't sure why. After the murder, I thought maybe it was to blame the death on Tank Wilson and Cortez."

Marvin and Elizabeth canceled the FBI agent flying into Riverview. The overheard conversation at the Cheaha Cabin changed the course of the investigation. But it was changed for the better. They were moving forward fast and furiously.

Initially, Hoss adamantly denied involvement in anything. He asked for an attorney. The attorney arrived at the jail within an hour. The agents advised him of their evidence against Hendricks and that his life could be in danger. Based on this information, and the promise of a reduced sentence, his attorney gave Hoss some good advice, cooperate!!

Hoss spilled the beans completely, practically tripping over his words. He and Jeff had initially met at the Funeral Home Convention in Vegas while gambling. They met Amanda while searching the dark web. Jeff had sold Hoss on the face replacement and selling organs. While on the dark web researching the business, they stumbled upon Amanda on a site for sociopaths, as JoAnn had predicted. He did not know about the cabin in Cheaha, only that Missy would disappear sometimes. However, he sensed something was amiss. Amanda had wholly taken over running the bank. She also had, to use his term, interfered with the operations of the funeral home. She had come on to him to get information. Hoss knew he was not attractive to her, which made him very suspicious. He also suspected she knew way more than she was letting on. Hoss insisted that Missy was utterly in the dark.

Three hours of interrogation by the agents revealed names of the participants in the Skin Game, surgeons in Atlanta who were performing the operations, and the admittance as an accessory to the murder of David Dingler.

"There was no stopping Jeff. I was totally against murder, but he was hell-bent on doing it. He had been planning this for over a year. It took him that long to find someone that resembled. He was even willing to change sexual persuasion to pull it off. A lot of people were threatening his life, and he wanted to disappear himself."

"When the plane comes in two days, we want you and Booley to meet it as normal," said Marvin. "We will make the arrests then. You know the people we are dealing with and what they are capable of; therefore, you will be taken to a safe house. I'm sure your life is in danger. You need us to help you keep from spending the rest of your life in prison, understand?"

"Yes," said Hoss.

"Where is Missy now?" asked Marvin.

"She said she and Amanda were going to Orange Beach for a few days and said she would call and let me know where they were staying. They asked me to go, but of course, she knew I would not. Never been a beach person."

Both Hoss and Zora were adamantly instructed not to communicate with each other, but to act normal when contacted by their partners in crime. They were both taken back to work and would be in separate safe houses until this went to court.

Chapter 51

The Plane

It was 2:30 in the morning on a Wednesday when the plane arrived. It taxied to a halt. Hoss and Booley carried the cargo toward the jet. The pilot had deplaned and was standing on the runway with the airport manager, James Smith.

Suddenly lights flooded the airport, and a loud siren sounded. A voice over a speaker said, "You are all under arrest. Lay down on the Pavement, face down with your arms outstretched." Everyone did as instructed, was cuffed, and helped to their feet.

After Miranda Rights were read to each one individually, all were escorted to the County Jail. Everyone except Hoss was locked up. He had been given immunity and was confined to a safe home.

The Mayor and City Council were notified mid-morning of the arrests. The City Attorney hastily recommended Booley's dismissal, and Booley was fired. As Billy Mac had hoped, Gene Lawrence was appointed temporary Chief of Police. He was called by Billy Mac, who congratulated him and invited him to a meeting that evening at JoAnn's. Gene eagerly accepted.

Chapter 52

Video Surveillance

Billy Mac got Marvin on the phone. "Marvin, the video is on at Cheaha. There are three people there right now, Missy Hendricks, Amanda Sistern, and I believe Jeff Thomas, complete with a new face."

"Where are you, Billy Mac, at JoAnn's?"

"Yes."

"I'm on my way." He picked up Elizabeth along the way.

JoAnn, Marvin, Elizabeth, and Billy Mac viewed the tape.

"We have to move now," said Marvin. He called and organized the FBI SWAT Team to surround the cabin. In two hours, they were at Cheaha.

Inside the cabin, Jeff Thomas heard rustling outside. He felt something wasn't right.

"Somebody is outside. I feel it. I want you two to leave by the front. I'm going out via the trap door. We need to move now."

Missy and Amanda went out the door and walked to their car. As they were getting in, Agents swarmed from everywhere. Jeff heard this and wasted no time. He went through the trap door in the kitchen and dropped to the crawl space. He kicked out the skirted area around the back and sprinted down the wooded hillside. He was out of sight before agents could get to the back.

Missy and Amanda heard their Miranda rights, were cuffed, put in a squad car, and on their way to jail in Riverview.

Billy Mac raced into the cabin, with two of the SWAT team members. Figuring Jeff, or whoever it was, left through the trap door.

Billy Mac did the same and, with agents in tow, raced down the steep wooded terrain.

Jeff reached the paved road below the cabin. He spotted a Yamaha Goldwing approaching. In a frantic mode, he stepped into the road and waved for the driver to stop.

He was screaming, "My wife, my wife, she's having a stroke, my car won't start!"

As the rider got off the bike, Jeff hit him full in the face with pepper spray. The guy screamed and stumbled into a ditch. Jeff was on the bike and gone. He knew he had to ditch this motorcycle quickly. He figured the authorities would find the guy he stole it from soon. There would be an APB out on within hours.

He was riding fast down Highway 431 South when he reached Lake Wedowee. He found an isolated part of the lake and pushed the bike into the water. Then he began walking. He had walked about a mile when he saw the car dealers' lot. He would have to be patient since they were still open. He waited until they closed, and it was dark.

He had decided to go for the new Chrysler Minivan at the back of the lot. Less of a chance of being seen. Plus, who would suspect a minivan? He hotwired it and headed toward Georgia. He decided to drive to Peachtree City. When he arrived, he checked into the Wyndham, safe for now. The minivan wouldn't be reported stolen until the morning.

Billy Mac and the FBI men found the motorcycle rider lying in a ditch on the side of the road. He relayed the story of what happened and gave a full description of his Goldwing.

Jeff had managed to escape temporarily. It was a terrible feeling knowing he was out there free, but they would find him. It was just a matter of when.

Chapter 53

Missy and Amanda

Elizabeth and Marvin interrogated Amanda, and Elizabeth took the lead. Unfortunately, Amanda wouldn't crack. Elizabeth later described the interview being like a second-team quarterback entering the game starting on your own three-yard line, down fifty to nothing.

No one could have budged Amanda. She refused to speak and asked to call her lawyer. She made a call to Texas.

Missy was a completely different story and caved on everything with no prompting. Marvin and Elizabeth interviewed her, again Elizabeth took the lead. Missy gave up some crucial additional information. She said one of the surgeons involved in the facial identity ring lived in Peachtree City, Georgia. He was an excellent golfer. She said he and Jeff played together at the Arnold Palmer Course there in Peachtree City. She knew this through her friendship with Amanda.

"What is the name of the surgeon?" asked Elizabeth.

"Dr. Benjamin Blakely. He has an office and a home in Peachtree City. But I don't know where the operations are done."

"Why, Missy? Why did you do this?" asked Elizabeth.

"I guess I was ashamed that my own flesh and blood could be so heartless. I know I didn't raise Amanda, so in all the years we were friends, I looked past her faults and made myself believe she loved me as I did her. When I found out what was going on, I wanted to hold my family together, even if I was the only one who cared. I, myself, am from a dysfunctional, broken family. Despite all my efforts, I have created another one. I have no excuses, besides wanting to be a part of my daughter's life, and to be rich, why else would I marry Hoss Hendricks. It was easy for Amanda to draw me into this mess. My desperation for a mother and daughter relationship made it easy. She's an outstanding actress."

After all the interviews were finished, a short meeting that night to inform Gene Lawrence. Marvin asked that both JoAnn and Billy Mac's homes were patrolled regularly. Gene agreed and said he would take care of it.

Chapter 54

Arnold Palmer Golf Course Peachtree City, Georgia

Agents in Atlanta were stationed at Arnold Palmer Golf Course and Benjamin Blakely's office. Billy Mac and FBI agents Holderfield and Duke drove to Peachtree City.

Jeff called a contact in Atlanta; he needed a tag and papers for the Minivan as well as a driver's license, etc. for his new identity. And he wanted it painted red. The man told him to bring $15,000 in cash. The papers would be ready that evening, but painting the minivan would take more than a couple of days. Jeff decided not to change the color. After all, he would have new plates and papers quickly enough and could disappear without a trace.

With a new identity and new wheels, the newly created Stephen Boyd called Ben Blakely. "How about golf tomorrow?"

"Sure, meet me at the first tee at 9 o'clock," said Dr. Blakely. "I'll need to tell the club who my guest is. Who should I tell them to expect?"

"Tell them, Stephen Boyd."

The next morning Marvin and Billy Mac were at the course. They saw a black Mercedes 550S pull in. That was the car Dr. Blakely usually drove, according to his receptionist. Of course, there were hundreds of 550Ss in Atlanta. Boom!! They hit the jackpot. Getting out of the car was none other than Dr. Blakely. They continued to watch him while he met "Jeff," and they began their round.

Billy Mac and Marvin were wearing greenskeepers tee-shirts and beige Bermuda shorts. They were feigning the repair of a part of the sprinkler system near the first tee. Both had on caps pulled low over their eyes. Billy Mac wore dark glasses.

The two men were hustling to the first tee. Sitting in the golf cart beside the Doctor was the man they suspected of being Jeff Thomas with his new face. That unquestionably was the man in the cabin.

Marvin spoke softly into a microphone and instructed two other agents to hustle to the green on the first tee.

The man they were sure was Jeff had just made a great shot to the green from the fairway and had a ten-foot birdie putt. He's one amazing guy, thought Billy Mac. In all this trouble, and he is out here, hitting great golf shots under pressure.

As he lined up his putt, Billy Mac turned and walked toward him.

"Hey, Bro. You're not playing enough break. You know what 'ole Sam Snead said, remember the three things he was scared of on a golf course; a downhill right to left putt, lightning, and Ben Hogan." Billy Mac laughed.

Jeff froze. The doctor said, "What in the hell is going on. We're playing for money, and you are in the way."

Marvin walked up to the doctor. "Dr. Benjamin Blakely, FBI, you are under arrest."

Jeff broke for the woods, confirming he was indeed Jeff. He was wearing golf shoes, not the best if you're running, the spikes are meant to dig into the ground. Billy Mack had on track shoes. He sped after him, and at the tree line of the rough, caught him, knocking him hard to the ground.

Quickly, Jeff got up winded, only to be smashed in the solar plexus hard, his breath left him as he fell to the ground. Billy Mac dragged him to a big pine tree. He pulled his arms around the tree and handcuffed him. There he was, captured, looking like he was tree-hugging.

The other two guys making up the foursome were held briefly for questioning, then released. They were simply shocked club members asked to be part of the foursome.

Billy Mac purposely did not want to talk to Jeff. He wanted him to sweat it out. He really didn't care if he ever talked to him again. He wanted to see JoAnn. He wanted to go home.

# # # #

The Wrap Up

JoAnn's house had never looked better as Billy Mac pulled in the driveway.

"I'm so proud of you, Billy Mac. You are incredible". They were in a long embrace, afraid to let go.

"JoAnn, after we wrap up tomorrow, or whenever we do it, I want us to go to 30A for a week."

"That's a wonderful idea."

# # # #

The Day After

The final meeting was held at JoAnn's. Attendees were Marvin Holderfield, Elizabeth Duke, newly appointed Police Chief Gene Lawrence, Sheriff Brian Langston, Pokey James, and Steve Sanders, DA. Marvin and Elizabeth summed everything up.

Marvin began, "I don't say this lightly, but you are an incredible bunch of people to work with, all of you, especially Billy Mac. Without you, sir, this never would have been solved. The FBI is working on rounding up those involved in the ring as we speak. Each one is eager to rat on the next. Congrats to you all!"

JoAnn started singing, "For he's a jolly good fella," They all joined in briefly before Billy Mac shushed them and shouted: "Last call for alcohol!"

Everyone laughed.

#

The Next Day

Billy Mac picked JoAnn up the next morning. He loaded her luggage in the back with his and got into the Tahoe. As they prepared to leave, Billy Mac's text went off. It was Pokey, "Love you guys, have fun. When you get back, have something really important to talk to you about."

No sooner had he read that text to JoAnn, in came text number two from Marvin. "Hope you guys have a great celebration and time off in 30A. When you get back, call me, I have something important to discuss with you, all good!"

They looked at each other and laughed. Then Billy Mac hit Apple car play. He had it loaded with songs, ones he and JoAnn loved and could sing along with. Mockingbird, James and Carly, Lou Rawls, James Brown, Andy Williams, Elvis, Sinatra, Johnny Cash, and don't forget Ella. That was just for starters.

And off they went, singing all the way to 30A.

Chapter 55

Fishing with John

The beauty of the emerald waters of 30A had a lingering effect on Billy Mac. He and JoAnn had been back for two days. But still, Billy Mac felt the need for more relaxation. Besides, he had some news to share. He made the call.

"Hello, John Underwood."

"Billy Mac at this end,"

"Hello, and how are you? I hear you guys had a great trip."

"We did. I was hoping I could cap it off with a little fishing trip to Lake Riverview with you. After all, you did promise to show me how to take a brim off the hook without getting finned."

"This old man would be honored. Those fish will be getting hungry about dusk. I'll bring the fishing gear, but you will have to bring the sardines, saltine crackers, be sure they are Nabisco Premium, hot sauce, and of course, some cold buttermilk. Can you handle that?"

"You bet I can! What time?"

"Six o'clock at the bridge behind the mall."

"See you then."

Billy Mac had his cooler loaded with supplies from Tank's butcher shop, complete with two small bags of ice. John would probably have another cooler full of ice, just in case they caught some fish. As he pulled up, John was waiting in his SUV, still in the driver's seat.

The smell of Lake Riverview wasn't pleasant, but it wasn't unpleasant. It was not the salty water and sand scent of the Emerald waters of 30A, but it made you feel alive. You knew you were at a river.

"Okay, we will set up here. It looks like we have some competition." John pointed to about a dozen ducks looking for food around the bank. They scattered when the folding chairs came out and were placed on the outer bank, about two hundred yards from the bridge.

John had brought some fine old fishing poles. He took the worms out and baited Billy Mac's pole for him. In about thirty seconds, Billy Mac saw the cork disappear underwater. He felt a sharp tug as the pole bent. As John had instructed, without jerking, he quickly pulled the fish out of the water. It was a dandy, a large bream. John, with a gloved hand, took the circle hook out of the fish's mouth with some long needle pliers. He then placed the fish back in the water at the bank's edge. As it became accustomed to the water, it swam back out in the lake again.

Billy Mac and John had decided to release all the fish they caught back into the water. John had explained that the more a fish had to fight, the more tired it would become; this would lessen their chance for recovery. That was why it was essential to get the fish out of and back into the water quickly.

Billy Mac was "hot." He was catching one fish right after another. He now could take the fish off the hook himself and let them back in the water.

"You are doing great," said John. It seems you're a natural at anything requiring coordination or athleticism, Billy Mac.

"Must be the teacher, and some good luck. John, have you and Vanessa ever thought about moving out of Riverview?"

"Sounds like you are fishing for something besides bream now, Billy Mac. This is me you're talking to. Why don't you just tell me what is on your mind?"

Billy Mac set his solo cup of buttermilk and his cracker with the sardine down and said, "Well, I guess I better do that, John. Has JoAnn mentioned the offers she and I have received in Atlanta?"

"Oh, yes! It sounds incredible for you both. Billy Mac, Atlanta is only two and a half hours away. It would take me two- and one-half years to explain to Vanessa why I moved her away from those tomato plants. I'm assuming you were asking us to move with you?"

In his best Denzel impersonation ever, he said, "Now, you see what I'm saying?"

Billy Mac laughed, "Yea, I do. But, I hope you know how I feel about you guys. It really makes this difficult for JoAnn and me."

Billy Mac's phone was vibrating. He reached in his pocket and saw JoAnn's name on the caller ID.

"It's your daughter. I better answer."

"What's up? I'm still out fishing with your dad."

"I'm at Brian's office with Marvin and Elizabeth. Jeff insisted he be taken to the office. David Dingler is also here. Jeff made a call that he should come to the Sheriff's office today. They are saying the body came from Benson Funeral Home. It was a corpse of a man who had died of a heart attack. There was no murder! Jeff wants you here and said he has information. Everyone wants you here now!"

Billy Mac told John he needed to get to the Sheriff's office immediately.

"I'll take care of loading the gear. Get on. It sounds like you have an urgent situation."

"Thanks, John! Will be in touch soon."

On the way to the Sheriff's office, Billy Mac called JoAnn.

"Tyrone at Partners and Booley Lancaster need to be summoned to identify Dingler."

"Yes, we have already done that. They are on their way. Booley is here already. He has been at a safe house, and the officers brought him here. He has already identified David Dingler. Tyrone is on his way."

"Great. Forgive me. I should have known you would take care of that, JoAnn."

"That's okay, no apologies needed. It's the way a great detective thinks, making sure of all the details. See you in a few."

Chapter 56

Sheriff's Office

Jeff said he would talk with Billy Mac and Holderfield, nobody else.

Billy Mac and Marvin entered the interrogation room. Nobody spoke. They sat down and fixed their gaze on Jeff.

Jeff began, "I guess a good place would be to start at the end and then back up. I was getting pressure from the Italian mob. There were some things about the operations and ring I knew that they didn't. Knowing these things would mean eliminating me and a whole lot more money for them. That's what was keeping me alive. I just kept stalling and trying to stay under the radar."

"What things?" asked Billy Mac.

"Names, places, and events, to be determined."

"The wise guys wanted me out. It was a matter of time before they found out all the connections. I knew as soon as they connected the dots, I was dead meat. So, I came up with a plan. I had to stage my death, but I wasn't sure how I would do it. When I heard about the party, I had the answer. I thought about killing David, but that would add murder to my resume. It was not smart. But what was smart was letting Hoss, Missy, and Amanda think that I had killed him, making them accessories to murder. It would ensure they kept their mouths shut."

"Then who put your face on what body?" asked Billy Mac.

"Cortez, He and I built my face just like the make-up artists do in Hollywood. Cortez didn't know what was going on beyond his job. He knew nothing about what I was planning. I just told him I wanted a new face, mine was getting wrinkled, and I had a young partner. The body came from Benson. He was a man who had died of a massive heart attack and had expressed his wishes to be cremated. It was just pure luck. He was about my skin tone and had hazel eyes. It was pure luck."

"Did Zora Benson know anything about this body?" asked Holderfield.

"No, they send bodies over frequently to be cremated. She suspected the organ ring but was never able to confirm her suspicions. Hoss managed to keep her in the dark about the face transplants. She did know Cortez was removing organs. Hoss said letting her know about it would keep her quiet."

"What about David Dingler? Where has he been, and what does he know?" asked Billy Mac.

"I gave him twenty-five thousand dollars to break up with me. I provided him with a prepaid cell and told him I would call him. He was advised that if he did not answer my call, it would put him in harm's way. He still has family in Cuba, and he knows I know where they are. As for where has he been? You will have to ask him. I don't know. I just told him to disappear."

"Jeff, did you know the Bureau was looking for you?" asked Marvin.

"Oh, yes! And that was just another reason to change my identity with this new mug I got. I must say, I didn't realize this new face would fuck with me as it has."

"Jeff, I hope you don't take this the wrong way. This face is not as good looking as the old Jeff face," Billy Mac said.

Jeff laughed. "You got me on that one, bro. But I'm getting better adjusted to it. Besides, it beats being dead. And it gives Agent Holderfield a chance to help me. So, Marvin, you help me; and I will help you.

"Marvin, maybe I should leave you two to discuss that," Billy Mac said.

"Oh, NO!" cried Jeff. "Bro, I want you to hear all this."

Marvin looked at Jeff and said, "I want you to hear it too, Billy Mac."

"Okay. I'll stay."

Marvin turned to Jeff and began, "Let me give you the likely scenario. It's not a guaranteed one, but a probable one.

Jeff, you are smart enough to know you will probably either serve jail time or be isolated somewhere in cow country. It all depends upon what we can work out with the federal prosecutor. Your testimony will be required at all the trials where your information is pertinent.

Now, just supposing for the sake of discussion, we get you in the Witness Protection Program. You would have to be isolated and monitored. What worries me, Jeff, is that it doesn't seem to mesh with your personality. Could you stay put? Even if you told us everything we wanted to know, named all the players, testified, and even if we did this for you, could you stay put? You wanna know what I think? Hell no! I don't think you could," said Marvin.

"Why would you even give a shit? The FBI gets the information it would take them years to accumulate. They catch all the bad guys and shut down the whole operation. Good publicity rains down from the heavens. Y'all would probably be hoping some hit man would find me and take me out. Maybe you could send the CIA to do it," laughed Jeff.

"Marvin, he may have a great point. I don't think I do give a shit," Billy Mac said.

"Well, I don't think I give a shit either, as long as we shut down this immoral operation," said Marvin.

They all laughed.

Chapter 57

Jeff's Fate

Another three hours produced details and information pertinent to the party and how the body fell. Jeff also spilled all the players involved he knew, and information about how the faceoff and organ ring was conducted.

Jeff told them that selling livers and other viable organs was a very lucrative part of the business. Jeff said it was unfortunate they called it body desecration. He admitted to being the one paying Billy Mac to follow people. But he said Hoss acted on his own in threatening Cortez and the attempted kidnapping of JoAnn. And yes, Amanda had known for twenty years that she was his and Missy's daughter.

When they got through, Marvin and Billy Mac got up to leave the room. Before walking out the door, Billy Mac stopped, turned around, and said to Jeff, "You know what, Jeff Thomas? You were one hell of a wide receiver."

"Thank you, Billy Mac!"

Marvin addressed the agents with him, "Prepare the prisoner for transport to a safe location."

Meanwhile, there was a traveler that had been en route to a new destination, a new city. There was a Glock in the travel bag in the overhead compartment on the bus. This quiet traveler had learned that the private bus line did not check onboard for weapons.

JoAnn greeted the interviewers as they left the interview room. She handed Marvin water with lemon and Billy Mac a diet Coke.

Two agents shackled and cuffed Jeff, who would be taken to an undisclosed safe house located in Atlanta. They were taking no chances with the man who would put an end to a horrific practice.

Billy Mac and JoAnn watched from the steps as Jeff was being led out of the Amicaclola County Courthouse toward a black SUV.

JoAnn's phone rang. The call was from Cleveland, Aunt Sophie.

"Hi, JoAnn, it's Sophie, dear. I'm quite worried! I just got back from vacationing with the girls in my Florida condo."

"Yes," said JoAnn as her eyes remained fixed on Jeff being led down the courthouse steps. "What's wrong, Sophie?"

"Amanda has escaped! She came by here and convinced Maria to give her a key to Jeff's place in the back. She was probably the only person Jeff ever genuinely cared about. I bet he told her about there being some money hidden in there. I'm not sure, but he may have also told her he had a gun there also to protect them from the bad guy. You know Anna believes people are trying to kill her."

Her voice trailed off as suddenly there was an explosive ear-deafening bang.

A girl sitting on the Courthouse steps sprung up and traveled fifteen feet in a hurry, raised a Glock, and blew Jeff Thomas' brains out.

Jeff saw her, and in an instant, he knew. She didn't know Jeff with the new face. He tried to say "virgin" their secret code, but the gunshot deafened his words.

Anna Thomas had just killed her brother.

As the Agents grabbed her, she laughed and kept saying over and over.

"I just killed the man that killed my brother. I just killed the man that killed my brother!"

JoAnn told Sophie she would have to call her back. "I'm sorry, so sorry to cut you off! There is an emergency; I need to get off the phone."

# # # #

Two Days Later

Pokey had hung around. He said his goodbyes and told Billy Mac and JoAnn to be in touch when they felt the need. He also reminded them of his standing invitation to visit Vegas. Marvin said the same thing, except about visiting Vegas.

"As tragic and bizarre as all of this has been," said JoAnn, "At least we have closure. Our part in this dreadful case is over, or maybe I shouldn't say that yet."

"We will see. We have all become very close, good friends," said Billy Mac. "I have a powerful feeling things will get a lot better for all of us and have no doubts we'll stay in touch."

"I have that same feeling, and I love you, man."

"I love you too."

Epilogue

The Irony of It All

Sometimes it is better just to allow events to happen rather than trying to change them. And sometimes people we care about the most hurt us the most. Too bad we can't ask Jeff Thomas what he thinks about that.

When our bodies start aging and our health may be failing, our spirit may be growing and taking us to new places. Anyone that has ever been in love knows that the energy we feel can take us to new heights. Just ask Billy Mac and JoAnn.

It is very unlikely Cortez Cortez and Greg Sistern will face prosecution. Everyone else, including Hoss, Missy, Amanda, Zora, Booley, and James Smith, will face some kind of punishment. Some will suffer a worse punishment, much more than others; some will face perdition.

Anna Thomas, having schizophrenia, will be declared mentally incompetent and not responsible for her actions. She will never be prosecuted but will spend time in a special kind of incarceration—her mind.

CPSIA information can be obtained
at www.ICGtesting.com
Printed in the USA
LVHW020423070721
691973LV00002B/124